"Above the mountains in the sky where clouds are formed, the heavens shine light to earth, and the presence of faith. Faith to believe in the beauty created by nature. Nature was created by the presence of 'the grass remembers them,' the horse."

By Anna Elizabeth

The Handbook of Horsemanship

Complete Handling/Training Resource Guide

By Anna Elizabeth Judd

Preface

Horsemen are exposed to inclement weather; hot summer heat, stinging sweat in the eyes, and spring mud up to the knees winter. Not to mention, breaking the ice on the water pails, snow falling, and ice storms. But, these inconveniences pale in comparison to the spiritual enlightenment received by spending every day with a horse.

Competent trainers have passion in their hearts for horses. Horsemanship is learned in a multitude of fashions, but guidance from an Equestrian Professional is the key to success. For example, I have had the privilege of being instructed by two world hall of fame trainers: Pete Kyle and Lighting Leonard Moore. They taught me the art of patience and perfection, two things that are a constant struggle when handling horses. Below is a literary reference that has given me insight when handling a horse.

"In any question of wisdom or prudence which the king put to them, he found them ten times better than all the magicians and enchanters in his kingdom."

Daniel 1; 20:

My goal in writing "The Handbook of Horsemanship" is to help anyone who reads the book to become a better horseman and to understand that training a horse is better done by using patience and perfection, not abuse.

In my vast years of training, there was one characteristic that remained consistent with horses, either young or old. Equus is a herd animal, therefore, the fight-or-flight instinct is the basis for survival. Training must follow the patterns of natural instincts. When the lessons stray, abuse becomes the foundation. Even though man domesticated Equus around 4000 B.C., there are sixty million years of evolution. Predispositions do not fade overnight.

Table of Contents

Chapter One

Evolution of the Horse

Origin

The early horse became known as the Dawn Horse; a small, fox-like, four toed animals about ten to twelve inches tall, which gradually evolved into the modern horse. This animal became classified as the Eohippus, which stems from the Greek words EO, meaning dawn and hippus, meaning horse.

Paleontologists found a distinctive trait that developed at different points in the evolution process that allowed them to identify the various Equine species, such as the presence of

the fossae (a shallow depression in the skull). This depression became quite detailed as the evolutionary process developed.

Plesippus is considered to be the animal between the eohippus and the modern-day horse, Equus. Equus stenonis, the true horse, was discovered in Italy.

Other species of wild horses were once indigenous to North America. They populated the continent before and during the last Ice Age. This occurred approximately 10,000 years ago. Some horses in the Western Hemisphere migrated to Eurasia across the Bering land bridge and fanned out from Siberia to the rest of Asia, Europe, and the Middle East. What horses remained in North America became extinct. There are several competing theories as to why this happened. One theory holds that climate changes associated with the end of the last Ice Age caused the extinction of the horse, the mammoth, and other large land animals. Another theory states that newly-arrived humans hunted horses to extinction. A third speculates that the newly arrived humans brought a biological factor that caused the demise of horses and other large ungulates in the Americas. However, all three may be contributing factors.

 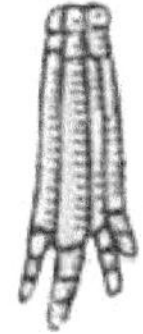

Re-population of the Equine in the Americas

When the Europeans came to the Americas with Christopher Columbus in 1492, they, of course, found no horses in the Western Hemisphere. Indigenous peoples of the Americas, Mexico, and Peru had no word for the animal since they had not seen any. They looked like a dog or deer to them, and in one case, horses were called "elk-dogs." In another tribe, they were known as the animal called "the grass remembers them," which was an ancestral memory dating back to the Ice Age.

When the missions were founded on the mainland, horses that had become lost or stolen started to populate feral herds. These feral horses became the Mustang and proliferated on the rich grasslands of North America. Some of their remains have been found in New Mexico and Wyoming.

Domestication of the Horse

It is unclear when horses were first domesticated, but cave art shows some depictions as early as 30,000 B.C. These were wild horses and most likely used for meat. The clearest evidence as a means of transport was found in 2000 B.C. However, new evidence supports domestication in Ukraine around 4000 B.C., although there has been a great deal of deliberation over the true meaning of domestication and what the definition entails. Therefore, domestication could have developed much sooner in the evolutionary tree.

Domestication of the Equine meant taming an animal who was an alert, swift, well-qualified leaper and jumper. They have the capability of eluding predators skillfully, despite their small brain capacity. By instituting selective breeding programs, the Equine has developed increased intelligence while retaining the genetic makeup that allowed them to become the awesome athletes they are today.

During the Ice Age, a number of the subspecies Equus ferus were used for meat. Evidence of numerous kill sites exists, and many cave paintings in Europe have allowed us to see what they looked like while in use.

Many students of horse domestication have problems accepting the fact that certain subspecies were apparently hunted to extinction by humans, especially in North America. Even though domestication became widespread in a short period, evidence shows some "wild" subspecies were found to be more suitable for taming and selective breeding, while others were left to be hunted, and some just died out.

After 8000 B.C., the horses in Europe most likely survived extinction because domestication had already begun with humans hunting feral herds and capturing other "wild" horses as livestock. Ironically, this was the approximate date of their extinction in the Americas. So, one could say that "domestic horses" existed in 8000 B.C.

Evidence of Equine domestication comes from the archaeological findings depicted horses used as mounts or draught animals. Additional information has been found in ceremonial burials that included types of equipment, tack, and Equine remains found in human graves.

The skeletal system of the horse has three major functions: protecting the vital organs, providing a framework, and supporting the soft parts of the body. Typically, horses have 205 bones. These bones are grouped into five categories according to their function: the long bones aid in locomotion, short bones absorb concussion, irregular bones protect

the central nervous system, sesamoid bones are embedded within a tendon, and the axial skeleton contains the skull, vertebral column, sternum, and ribs. The sternum consists of multiple sternebrae that fuse to form one bone, attaching to the ten "true" pairs of ribs out of eighteen ribs total.

Appendicular Skeleton

The appendicular skeleton includes the fore and hind limbs. Attached to the vertebral column via the pelvis are the hind limbs. The horse's front limbs attach with tendons and muscles directly to the spine (horses do not have a collar bone).   This allows for a shoulder angle of one hundred twenty to one hundred thirty degrees when standing, which can extend to one hundred forty-five degrees and flexing to an eighty-degree angle, therefore enabling the horse to raise the front legs over an obstacle such as jumping.

The following are the bones in the forelimb starting at the withers. The scapula (shoulder blade) is a flat bone that partially forms the withers and is one of the integral points in determining a horse's conformation. The humerus lies between the scapula and radius, forming a fifty-five-degree angle down the back. The radial bone extends from the elbow and travels down to the carpus and forms the forearm of the horse. The ulna caudal to the radius is partially fused in adult horses. The shoulder joint (scapulohumeral joint) or elbow is a hinged joint that can flex fifty-five to sixty degrees. Finally, the carpus (knee) consists of seven to eight bones placed in two rows to form three joints. However, the first carpal bone is missing fifty percent of the time. Bones of the lower limbs are present in both front and hind legs, although they vary in length. The difference creates a five-degree steeper angle in the hindquarters than the front legs. Seven bones form the lower legs: the cannon bone, splint bones, proximal sesamoid bones, long pastern, short pastern, coffin bone, and navicular bone.

Attached to the hind limbs is the pelvis. Made of os coxae, it is the largest flat bone in the horse. It is larger in mares to accommodate more room for the foal during birth. The femur is the longest bone in the horse and is located proximally (nearer the center of the body). This forms a ball-and-socket joint with the pelvis and the hip joint. The patella distally (away from the point of attachment) meets the tibia at the stifle joint. The tibia runs from the stifle to the hock. The stifle joint (femoropatellar joint) is composed of three joints stabilized by a network of ligaments with an angle of about one hundred fifty degrees. The tarsus, or hock, consists of six bones fused with the 1st and 2nd tarsal bones aligned in three rows. The calcaneus (human heel) creates the tuber calcis, to which the tendon of the gastrocnemius, portions of the biceps femoris, and portions of the deep flexor tendon attach.

Thoracic Vertebrae

The thoracic vertebrae (the back) are an integral part of the usefulness of the horse. Its a complex design of bone, muscle tendons, and ligaments all working together to support the weight of a rider? The structure of the back varies immensely from breed to breed, along with the age and condition of each animal. There is an average of eighteen thoracic vertebrae, with five located in the withers alone.

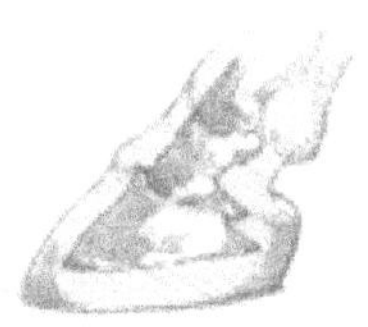

Horses have no collar bone; therefore, the entire torso is attached to the shoulders by the following powerful muscles. The longissimus dorsi is the longest and strongest muscle in the horse and is located under the rider and saddle. The supraspinous ligament begins at the poll (top of the head, between the ears) and ends at the croup (sacral

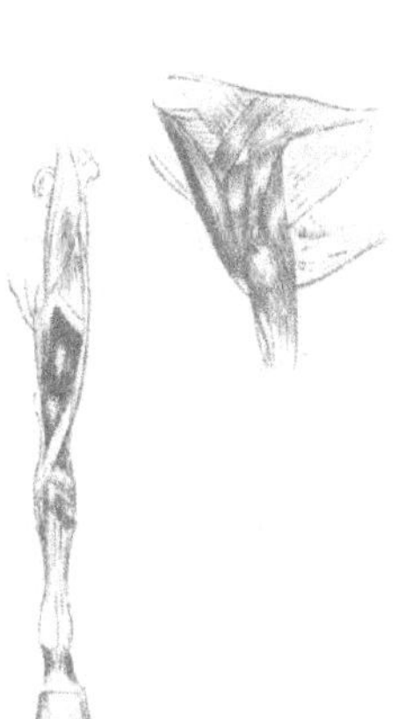

vertebrae), supporting the head and neck. The nuchal ligament supports the withers and neck. Equines should have a short back and a relatively long underline for ideal confirmation.

The smoothness of gait, ability to collect, and agility depend on the length of the back. One of the areas of concern to a horseman is the withers, which can affect the length of stride, shoulder movement, and how well the saddle fits the horse.

Odd-Toed Ungulates

The modern horse belongs to the order known as the Perissodactyls, or "odd-toed ungulates." They all share hoofed feet and an odd number of toes on each foot. Early ancestors of the horse walked on several spread-out toes, which was an accommodation to a life spent walking on soft, moist grounds of primeval forests. Through evolution, modern Equine predecessors needed to be capable of greater speed to outrun predators. Therefore, this was attained through the lengthening of limbs and lifting of some toes from the ground in such a way that the weight of the body was gradually placed on one of the longest toes, the third.

Equine Hoof

At birth, foals' front and hind feet are identical, but dramatic changes occur as they become adults. The horse hoof is made of an anterior part called the hoof capsule (composed of various cornified specialized structures), which protects and supports the P3 bone, also known as the coffin bone. The posterior part covers and protects delicate soft tissues,

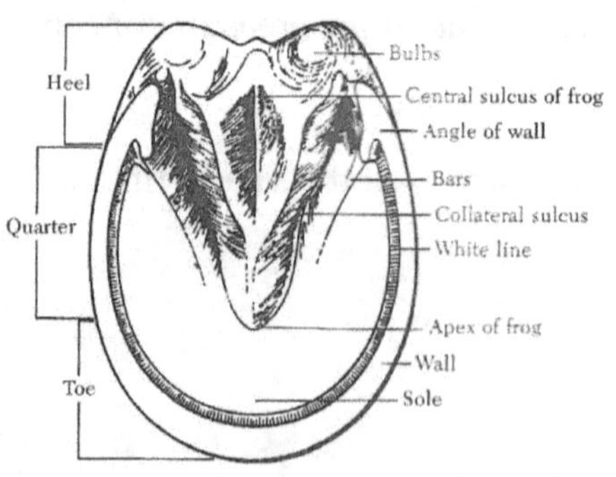

tendons, ligaments, fibro-fatty and/or fibrocartilaginous tissues, and cartilages. The upper, almost circular limit of the hoof capsule is the coronet band. It has an angle to the ground of roughly similar magnitude in each pair of feet. These angles will vary from one foot to another, but not markedly. The heels are separated by an elastic structure called the frog. The frog is dark gray-blackish in color and has a rubbery consistency, suggesting its role as a shock absorber and grip tool on hard or smooth ground. In stable horses, the frog does not wear. However, it can degrade with bacterial and fungal activity, becoming irregular and having a slashed surface known as thrush. It is treatable with proper care.

Beneath the rear of the sole, there is the distal cushion separating the frog and bulbs of the foot from underlying tendons, joints, and bones. This distal cushion provides impact protection. In foals, the distal cushion is composed of fibro-fatty tissue, and as the foals mature, it turns into fibrocartilaginous tissue. The hoof will stay healthy with a sufficient, consistent concussion to stimulate the back of the hoof. Normal transformation of the digital cushion into fibrocartilaginous tissue is now considered to play a key role in both the prevention of navicular syndrome (inflammation or degeneration of the navicular bone and its surrounding tissues) and the rehabilitation of recovering case

The Hoof Mechanism

 The horse hoof is elastic and flexible, allowing it to physically change shape to the variable depth of 1-1.5 cm due in part to the arched shape of the wall and sole. When weight is applied to the frog, it is compressed vertically and expands laterally into the sole and bars. The coffin bone descends into the hoof capsule, slightly compressing the solar corium around the solar border of the coffin bone. When the hoof is depressed, diastolic phase blood is pushed into the wall's corium. When uploaded, the hoof contracts, and blood is squeezed out, assisting in circulation and dissipating shock.

Stay Apparatus

Since horses live life as prey animals, a "stay apparatus" developed in their legs. This ability allows them to stand while they sleep without collapsing. Horses do not need solid sleep, just many short periods of rest, an average of four to fifteen hours of standing sleep, and a few minutes to a few hours lying down. To reach REM sleep, they must lie down for an hour or two every few days. However, if the horse cannot lie down after several days, it will become sleep deprived and may suddenly collapse as it involuntarily falls into REM sleep.

To maintain normal healthy sleep patterns, horses must have at least 2 ½ hours of REM sleep every twenty-four hours. The age of the horse and their physical health will determine the amount of lying down they do. Depending on the horses' housing environment, they will usually take turns sleeping while one horse stands guard.

Brain Capacity

Compared to the size of the brain and body mass of the horse, it is hard to believe the Equine is so easily trainable, even though their reasoning abilities are extremely limited. However, the horse has one outstanding asset: a well-developed cercbcllum that controls its sense of balance. The relation between terrain and foot placement is acute.

When an animal is not able to reason, its interpretation of a situation is limited. For example, Equines associate fear with objects, not people or environments. Even with these disabilities, the horse's superb athletic ability, combined with their willingness to please and sensitivity to touch and pressure, makes them the most trainable of the large, domesticated animals.

Another well-developed asset of the horse is the highly sensitive nerve connections in their hair follicles. This enables a sensory perception that allows the horse to feel insects landing on their skin. That extends to the hairs on the muzzle. The prehensile lips allow them to taste and determine the nature of the plants they are eating. For this reason, horses generally will not eat toxic plants when ample healthy food is available.

Equine Vision

Equine vision has a unique combination of monocular and binocular sight. The horse has a visual acuity of 20/33, slightly worse than most humans. In their retina, there is a linear shape called the visual streak, an area that allows the horse to have better acuity (clarity). However, this forces them to tilt, raise, and lower their head to help clarify objects.

These two types of vision cannot be used at the same time. Like most prey animals, horses' eyes are set on the sides of their head, giving them a three-hundred-forty-degree range of monocular vision. As a result, most horses are exceptionally sensitive to motion since motion is usually the first alert of a predator's approach. However, this condition also gives them two blind spot areas where the animal cannot see. These are directly in front and directly behind the body (making a cone

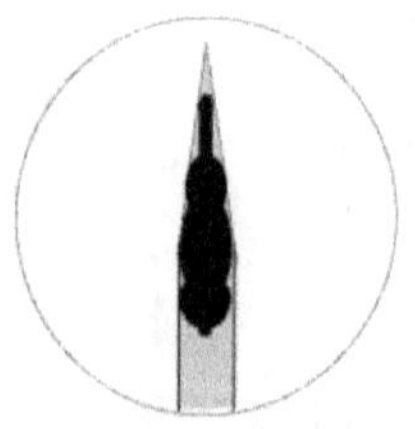

shape that forms a triangle three to four feet in front of the horse's face, directly behind the head following their back,

and extending behind the tail). This eliminates their binocular vision to about sixty-five degrees.

Binocular vision allows the use of both eyes to focus on an object. For this reason, they must raise or lower their head to focus their vision, limiting their depth perception. Therefore, handlers must allow plenty of time for their eyes to adjust when entering locations with drastic light changes, such as barns, horse trailers, water holes, ponds, lakes, streams, rivers, etc. An instinct for the horse in this situation, since their eyes do not focus swiftly, is to paw with their foot, allowing them to judge the depth of the object they are being asked to enter. Such a situation might include a horse that is being asked to "collect" while riding. This lowers their field of vision, making them less able to focus on distant objects. Jumping horses, for example, will raise their head before they jump, enabling them to assess the proper take-off spot.

Color Vision

For many years, scientists have studied the idea of horses seeing color. In recent years it has been proven that Equines have dichromatic vision. In the visual wavelengths of light, there are three colors: blue, green, and red. Horses can see any variation of blue and green light, but they cannot see red or any other deviation of red. This may be due to horses being most active at dawn and dusk.

 In the eye, there are rods and cones, which are responsible for converting light into impulses that are transmitted to the brain for interpretation. Horses have a higher proportion of rods to cones, as well as a tapetum lucidum (a layer of cells in the wall of the eye of nocturnal animals). This gives them enhanced vision in low-light conditions. However, they cannot adjust to light changes quickly, and this should be taken into consideration by the horseman. For instance, give the horse plenty of time to enter a barn, horse trailer, or anywhere the light changes are dramatic.

 Among land animals, a horse has the largest eyes and relies heavily on them, just as we do. Eye disorders in horses that are similar to those in humans include corneal abrasions, corneal ulcers, moon blindness, glaucoma, and many others. During the seasons of the year when insects are the most prevalent, using a fly mask is advisable. When an eye injury occurs, immediate attention from a veterinarian may be necessary. Changes in normal color, clarity, or swelling indicate the need for a veterinarian.

Equine Hearing

Like all animals, including humans, horses have binaural (perception of sound by both ears) hearing. The ears can hear sound concurrently (at the same time). A horse's external ears are known as pinnae. They act like satellite dishes to capture sound waves and funnel them to the inner ears. Because of the large cuplike shape of the pinnae, especially when compared to humans' small flat ones, very little sound spills out of them. This allows the horse to capture noises you might miss.

Equines can hear a wider range of high-frequency tones, such as the ultrasonic squeak of a bat. For a prey animal, this hearing acuity makes sense. In their natural environment, other animals, including predators, are the only things besides weather that generate noise. Predators generally don't vocalize when stalking prey, so the horse is hard-wired to listen for the sounds of stealth: for example, the snap, crackle and pop of grass and twigs.

These telltale rustlings contain high-frequency sounds, which the horse uses to locate direction using something called gauging. Unlike animals that can hone in on a precise location, horses need only an approximate indication of where the sound erupted. If the sound necessitates action, they will follow with eye movement, then finally raise and turn their head to focus better. This is followed by freezing the body, so as not to give away their position. This causes them to stop chewing, eliminating noise, and finally, if warranted, they make a quick getaway.

 Again, to reiterate, due to horses' limited reasoning abilities, they have a heightened emotional response to whatever sensory input they might perceive as a danger. This instinct initiates the first survival mechanism: flight.

Olfactory System

The horse's olfactory receptors (sense of smell) are located in the mucosa of the upper nasal cavity. Due to the length of the nasal cavity, there are a large number of receptors. In addition, horses have a vomeronasal organ in the hard palate (the anterior bony portion) of the mouth. This enables them to pick up pheromones and other scents, exhibiting the flehmen response (from German flehmen, meaning curl the lip). The flehmen response forces air through splits in the nasal cavity into the vomeronasal organ and causes them to make a snorting sound.

Equine Reproduction

All foals born are known as fillies (females) or colts (males). At the age of four, fillies are now mares, and colts are stallions. However, a castrated stallion is called a gelding. The castration can be done as early as eighteen months, provided the testicles have dropped.

Mare Reproduction

The mare's reproductive system is responsible for controlling gestation, birth, lactation, and heat cycles. They have two ovaries, as with most mammals. The ovaries generally tend to decrease in size as the mare ages. Fillies reach puberty at twelve to fifteen months and begin an estrous cycle of every twenty-one to twenty-three days. Cycles last an average of seven to ten days.

The uterus is about twenty to twenty-five centimeters, and she has two mammary glands which open externally between the hind legs. Pregnancy lasts for approximately three hundred and thirty-five to three hundred forty days, normally resulting in one foal; twins are rare. Lactation lasts about six to eight months, depending on the size and development of the foal. Normally foals are weaned from the mare by eight months, and four to six months is the preferred time.

Stallion Reproduction

Stallions have two testicles and a penis with a urethral fossa (the sheath) at the distal end of the organ. Stallions' and geldings' sheaths must be checked regularly for a waxy substance caused by dirt and dead skin cells in the sheath. Geldings are more prone to this problem than stallions because castration limits the number of microorganisms in the sheath pocket. Cleaning the sheath should be done once or twice a year. A dirty sheath can be extremely painful and even inhibit performance. This is not a medical procedure and can be performed by anyone. Your local veterinarian can teach you the procedure.

Herbivorous Teeth

During the evolution of the Equine, their teeth have undergone significant changes. They started as original omnivorous teeth: very short and even bumpy. The molars

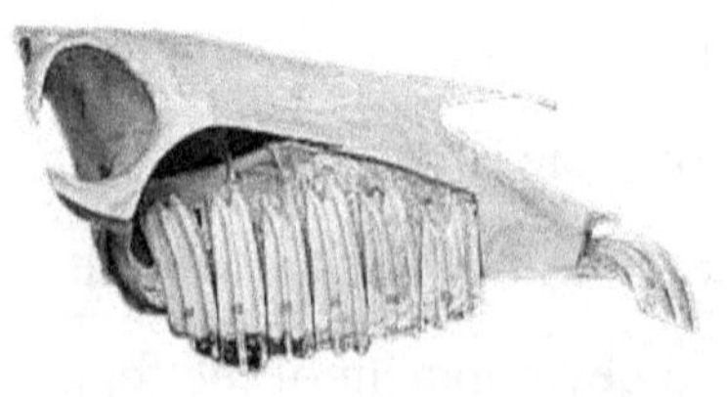

gradually changed themselves into the molars of herbivorous mammals.

An adult horse has between thirty-six to forty-four teeth, and all horses have twelve premolars, twelve molars, and twelve incisors. They also have between four and five canine teeth that come in between the molars and incisors. Generally, canine teeth are found in only male horses; less than twenty-eight percent are found in female horses. "Wolf" teeth are vestigial premolars found between the molars and incisors normally in the upper jaw, and for this reason, they are pulled to limit interference with the bit. Contrary to popular belief, the bit is not held between the horse's teeth but lies in the inter-dental space that lacks teeth. About thirteen to twenty-eight percent of all horses born only have one or two wolf teeth. Equine teeth continue to grow about one-eighth inch each year. Horses use mastication to wear their teeth.

Foals' teeth begin to emerge at six to ten weeks in regular intervals after birth until the age of five. These teeth are only caps below the gum line. In some cases, these caps become impacted in the gum or get wedged against other teeth, causing performance issues. This normally is only a temporary problem until the adult teeth emerge; once the caps have come off, the problem should fix itself. If the horse show signs of discomfort, veterinarian care may be necessary.

Like humans, horses have dental problems as well. These problems are related to the fact that their teeth continue to grow throughout their lives. Their teeth were designed to wear against the lower tooth while chewing, preventing growth. Many times, the teeth wear unevenly, causing spurs that interfere with jaw motion. These spurs can be very painful and can even cut the horse's cheeks. Wild horses' natural foodstuffs may have been rougher forages than the modern horse and ground their teeth better. The lusher and softer forages, as well as grain, reduce the natural wear of the teeth. For this reason, they should be checked in the fall and spring once the horse has matured at the age of five. The following list is some of the signs of dental problems, not only the physical signs but performance problems as well.

Physical Problems

> ➤ Reluctance to eat, or eating slowly.
> ➤ Dull coat, weight loss, and loss of energy.
> ➤ Quidding (dropping food partially chewed while chewing).
> ➤ Turning the head while eating.
> ➤ Excessive salivation, or blood in salivation.
> ➤ Foul smell from mouth or nose.
> ➤ Discharge from one nostril.
> ➤ Undigested feed in manure.
> ➤ Colic.
> ➤ Facial swelling.
> ➤ Performance Problems

➢ Head tossing.

➢ Gaping at the mouth.

➢ Refusal to pick up and carry a bit properly.

➢ Difficulty picking up a canter on the correct lead or performing flying lead changes.

➢ Refusal to collect.

➢ Bucking, running off, and refusing to take the bit when bridling.

Digestive System

Horses have evolved as grazing animals, eating small amounts at a time and traveling significant distances each day to obtain adequate nutrition. As a result, their digestive system is about one hundred feet long, most of that being intestines.

Digestion begins in the mouth, where there are four pairs of salivary glands. Next is the esophagus, which is about five feet in length. From there, the esophagus enters the stomach at an acute angle. This creates a one-way valve with a powerful sphincter mechanism at the gastroesophageal junction, which is why horses cannot vomit.

The next digestive organ is the stomach, which is relatively small compared to its size. The average horse has a stomach with a capacity of four gallons and works the best at about half full. Remember, the horse developed, consuming small amounts of food and moving consistently. Thus, feeding the horse several small meals a day is highly recommended. Their stomach empties at two-thirds full, whether the contents have been processed or not. Feeding a horse two large meals a day prevents them from utilizing all the nutrients in their feed.

Once the stomach empties, the food goes into the small intestine, which is fifty to seventy feet long and has a ten to twelve-gallon capacity. Most of the nutrients are absorbed here. The large intestine is known as the "water gut," where any remaining liquids and roughage go. It holds about seven to eight gallons and is approximately four feet long. It contains bacteria that feed on cellulose plant fiber. This is why changing a horse's feed must be done gradually, allowing the bacteria time to adapt. Quick changes can cause colic and improper digestion.

The large colon, small colon, and rectum make up the remainder of the large intestine. The first part of the large intestine is the large colon. About ten to twelve feet long, it can hold up to twenty gallons of water. There are several twists and turns as it leads to the small colon. Due to these twists and turns, it is commonplace for the horse to experience colic from an impaction. The remainder of the large intestine ends with the small colon. Ten to twelve feet long, it only holds five gallons; this is where the majority of water in the horse's diet is absorbed. It is also where fecal balls are formed. Measuring a foot long is the rectum, a chamber where the waste matter is expelled from the body.

Respiratory System

The respiratory system, just as in man, consists of the nostrils, pharynx, larynx, trachea, diaphragm, and lungs. The respiratory system not only allows the horse to breathe but also forms an important part of the horse's olfactory (smell) system.

At a resting rate, the horse has respiration of approximately twelve to thirty-two bpm (breaths per minute). The Equidae family has a unique part of the respiratory system called the guttural pouch, which is thought to equalize the air pressure in the tympanic membrane (the eardrum). These are left and right membranes located between the mandibles, below the occiput; they are each capable of holding three hundred to five hundred ml of air when the horse swallows or exhales.

The larynx guards the entrance of the trachea, stopping the aspiration of foreign objects and regulating the flow of air. A cartilage trap between the larynx and trachea is the epiglottis, which closes the air passage when food is swallowed.

The trachea carries about seventy-five to eighty centimeters of air through the oral cavity to the lungs. It is held permanently open by fifty to sixty centimeters. The lungs are located in the thoracic cavity, which, when fully expanded, can reach the 16th rib.

Circulatory System

A unique characteristic of the Equine is something that only recently has been acknowledged. The distal limb of the Equine has an extensive musculature system surrounding the leg, and the smooth muscle appears to be under neural control. In the distal leg, the veins pulsate like arteries.

Veins and Arteries

The veins and arteries carry blood throughout the body via the heart. Arteries are thick-walled, muscular vessels that carry the blood away from the heart. These vessels branch, decreasing in size, and proliferate to become arterioles and finally become capillary beds. Capillaries unite to form small veins, and these veins combine to form large veins that return blood to the heart. Pulmonary arteries carry the oxygen-poor blood to the lungs from the heart, and enriched blood is returned to the heart by the pulmonary veins.

Lymphatic System

The lymphatic system is an assistant to the circulatory system and forces nutrients and fluid into the tissues. Not all the fluid returns via the venous system; the remainder is picked up through the thin-walled lymph vessels.

The Heart

Weighing an average of 8.5 lb., the horse's heart has four chambers, just like in humans. The cardiac muscle has but one job: pump blood through the body. An Equine heart grows until the age of four years. It increases in size slightly with proper conditioning, but the size does not directly correlate to the size of the horse. On average, the heart pumps nine gallons of blood per hour in a thousand-pound horse.

In the 1700s, an excellent producer of broodmares was a horse known as Eclipse. He had eighteen starts and eighteen wins. Eclipse was the first horse to be documented with the "X" factor. He had an enlarged heart weighing fourteen pounds. Phar Lap, Sham, and Secretariat all had hearts weight twenty-two pounds each. It was also thought the great-producing mare Pocahontas was homozygous for the "X" factor as well. Homozygous means having a pair of identical alleles at corresponding chromosomal loci. Such a horse can produce only one kind of germ cell for that trait. Large hearts can be traced back for four generations of her pedigree, eventually leading to Eclipse. This pedigree can be found in several famous horses, including Princequillo, War Admiral, Blue Larkspur, and Mahmound. The "X" chromosome can only be passed through to a stallion's daughter. The dam can pass through a colt or filly.

Survival Instincts

This small fox-like creature endured the struggle for survival for sixty million years. This survival resulted in two basic forms of instincts; flight or fight behavior. These prominent behaviors are explained below.

Flight: The flight mechanism is the horse's primary response to survival.

These senses are activated when any danger is perceived by the horse. Danger can range from a wild predator such as a cougar or bear, or the handler asking the horse to perform a task that is unfamiliar or unnatural to them. In response to the fear, the horse will flee to a position in which he re-enters his comfort zone. It is usually a distance in which he is removed from the impending danger.

Fight: The fight mechanism is the horse's second order of survival.

The horse relies mainly on its natural ability to run, except in situations when flight is not possible. Several behaviors will emerge when fleeing a situation, such as rearing, kicking, or biting. These are some of the more common responses; however, when the horse is restrained, other behaviors could occur: for example, bucking, striking, throwing their head, and pawing. Such behaviors will continue until one of two things happen. Either the horse is removed from the restraints, or they become comfortable with their situation. Although if continued restraint is used on a fearful horse, they will not learn to control their anxiety correctly.

Herbivore Herds

In herbivore herds, there are "pecking orders." These pecking orders are separated into two groups of horses: dominant and subordinate. Below is an explanation of both types of horses.

Dominant: The dominant allele of a gene pair; ruling or controlling; having or exerting authority.

Subordinate: Place in or belonging to a lower-ranking order.

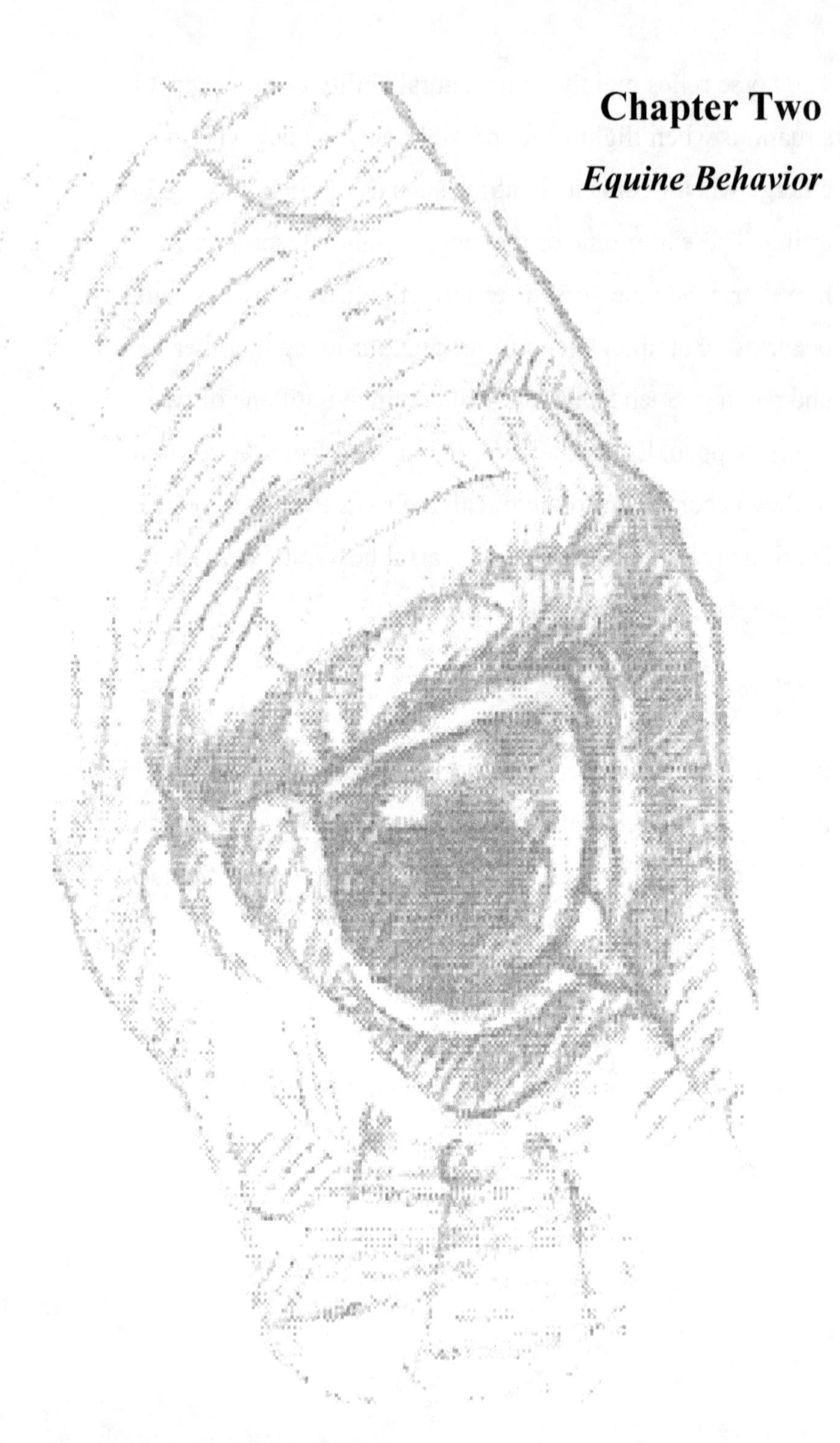
Chapter Two
Equine Behavior

On Horsemanship

"If a rider signals the horse to gallop off and holds him back at the same time, the horse will collect himself and raise his chest and forelegs. This will not be with natural suppleness because the horse is annoyed by the restraint. However, if a horse's fire is kindled and the rider relaxes the bit, the horse will move forward with pride, a stately bearing, and pliant legs. They will not be willing but will show themselves off in the greatest of grandeur spirited beauty."

The above statement written by Xenophon in 350 B.C. is one of the earliest treatises (a systematic exposition in writing of the principles of a subject) written in the Western World. Xenophon (a Greek general) himself pays tribute to a better-established work by a celebrated horseman known only as "Simon." Unfortunately, no known copies exist in the modern world.

These training techniques included the principles of classical dressage in a manner that is non-abusive and is stilled followed today. To better explain the idea behind these principles is the literary quote from John 3; 6:8.

"What is born of the flesh is flesh and what is born of spirit is spirit. Do not be amazed that I told you, 'You must be born from above.' The wind blows from where it will, and you can hear the sound it makes, but you do not know where it comes from or where it goes; so, it is everyone who is born of the spirit."

Social Behavior

Selective breeding programs have bred the Equine to be quite docile, especially the large draft horse. In recent years, lightweight breeds are now being bred for speed, agility, alertness, and endurance. Therefore, understanding Equine behavior is essential to proper management.

Like all creatures, horses' social behavior developed to ensure survival. Modifying the horse's behavior through domestication has left many horsemen with limited knowledge of what normal and abnormal behavior is. The list below is the nine categories grouped to classify Equine behavior.

Contractual behavior is generally considered the result of seeking affection or protection from another horse, such as huddling together during inclement weather or in times of suspected danger.

Ingestive behavior is the act of ingesting food or water. The horses' anatomy and physiology are designed to eat small amounts of food at one time and graze over large areas, moving constantly. This consequently makes the horse susceptible to digestive disorders caused by overeating in short periods.

Eliminative behavior is the activity of urination or defecation. Most horses will establish an elimination area in the paddock or stall and normally avoid that area until there is no other source of food. Most adult horses will avoid feces of their kind. However, foals repeatedly eat the mare's feces when placed in dry lots. Coprophagy (feeding on feces) in adult horses is abnormal behavior. This behavior can be caused by a nutrient imbalance, usually low levels of protein. Although this is not always the case, sometimes it can be due to boredom. Purchasing toys for your horse may be helpful during idle times between feedings. Another option would be feeding the horse several small meals during the day.

In general, this eliminative behavior develops habits in each horse, such as routinely defecating in stressful situations or when put back in a stall or paddock.

Sexual behavior includes all acts associated with the fertilization process, including courtship and copulation. Geldings may also elicit sexual behavior if they reach adult maturity before castration.

Epimeletic behavior is the giving of care and attention between a mare and a foal. Other epimeletic behaviors may include mutual scratching, especially over the withers of each horse, or standing head to tail to fight flies.

Et-Epimeletic behavior is a strong social bond. This is commonly seen when horses are separated, especially foals from mares. When weaning a foal from the damn, the best process is the duration of the full moon. Weaning foals at this time will diminish strong et-epimeletic behavior. At times, this strong social bond finds many horsemen in distress when having to deal with a barn sour horse. et-epimeletic behavior can be witnessed best during feeding times. These common erratic temperaments include pawing, aggression toward other horses as well as the handler, kicking, biting, or any other dangerous outburst. Most stall vices also develop due to et-epimeletic behavior.

Allelominetic behavior is the act of mimicry. This type of behavior is referred to as contagious or infectious by some horsemen. Horses housed together will sometimes mimic behaviors such as running in a paddock or pasture, normally from suspected danger. Foals will run and play simply because the others are. Sometimes horses that are grouped in herd situations become difficult to catch and most likely cause a chain reaction with the rest of the herd. Also another allelominetic behavior is cribbing (the act of chewing wood or sucking air).

Investigative behavior is the sensory perception of their environment and is behavior that is highly developed in the Equine species. Generally, this perception involves movement, sight, touch, smell, hearing, and sometimes taste. Due to the diminished vision of the Equine, the horse is very seldom satisfied to investigate a new object by sight alone. As a result, the investigative behavior must be completed before a horse will accept something new without continuous apprehension. Signs of the sensory response can be seen best when the horse is asked to perform tasks unfamiliar to them, such as trailer loading, saddling, or crossing water. On occasion, this behavior can be the reason a horse becomes difficult to catch.

Agonistic behavior is a linear ladder that starts from the most dominant horse to the most submissive herd member. This hierarchy is established through aggression to prevent severe fighting. Then, as long as the same horses stay together, only the threat of aggression is needed. Threats may include pinning the ears, baring their teeth, and sudden movements toward another horse. However, other variables like size, maturity, home territory, old age, and injury can mask the dominance hierarchy.

Sometimes, horses that appear dominant in a stall can be submissive in a herd environment and vice versa. This is known as a false expression of dominance. These false expressions usually occur when food is present in a feeder or manger. Therefore, it is best to group horses with closely related temperaments, to minimize fighting or injury. Careful supervision must happen during the period these herd situations are taking place. When a submissive horse is forced into such a stressful state, colic can be induced. It can even cause stall vices to develop over short periods. To help eliminate such stresses, the submissive horse should be allowed plenty of room for retreat and not be forced to stand and fight. In most cases, the horses will establish a balance in the hierarchy ladder on their own. But they should be watched closely for the duration of the conflict, as separation may be needed permanently. If at all possible, let the horses resolve this conflict on their own without interference from any humans. Horses do learn to live together without serious conflict.

The idea behind Equine behavior is a very complicated topic, and it takes many years to learn the normal and abnormal behaviors of the horse. The best way to understand why your horse reacts the way he or she does is to watch their everyday behaviors. This will allow you to understand when an abnormal behavior occurs

Chapter Three
Stall Vices

Stall Vices

Stall vices (depraved behavior) are neurotic behaviors that begin in unnatural living conditions. Most vices start due to boredom, hunger, excess energy, isolation, and sometimes allelominetic behavior (mimicry of other horses). Numerous negative health effects can be caused by long-term vices.

Nearly all vices occur in animals confined to small quarters on a full-time basis. The best form of therapy is full-time turn out in a pasture or large paddock. Over several weeks and months, most of the problems will diminish. However, they may never be fully rehabilitated. Stall vices are rarely seen in pastured horses because it is a natural living environment.

The list below is some typical stall vices that occur in horses confined to small housing environments:

Wood chewing is gnawing wood caused by hunger or boredom and may eventually lead to a more severe vice known as "cribbing." This is when a horse puts their mouth on a fence rail or board, arches its neck, and sucks air. Cribbing eventually leads to colic and tooth damage. In many cases, endorphins (brain opiate receptors released in the body due to stress or trauma) are released in the body, causing the horse to become addicted to the behavior, similar to someone who smokes cigarettes.

Weaving has been known as the racehorse vice because of its commonality on the race track. Weaving is the action of swaying from side to side, swinging the head back and forth. It develops in horses that are stall bound and nervous, possibly a self-stimulating behavior. Weaving can cause weight loss, uneven hoof wear, and stress on the lower legs.

Wall kicking is usually caused by boredom and lack of exercise. It is likely a learned habit by watching other horses. Kicking with the hind legs causes potential injury to the horse, as well as damage to the barn.

Biting is a nervous, anxious habit, also caused by being stall bound. Box stalls are normally designed with bars to keep the horse from putting its head out of the stall. This form of biting is the reaction a horse will exhibit essentially as a form of getting attention.

Circling (pacing) is a repetitive motion where the horse makes circles in the stall instead of rocking back and forth. It eventually leads to weight loss and lameness.

Pawing is digging with the front feet. Horses that paw can cast themselves in the fence. They can also dig large holes in the stall floor and place uneven stress on the legs and feet.

There are several ways to diminish the reoccurrences of stall vices and or eliminate them altogether. Just keep in mind that once a severe stall vice has been established by a horse, the chances of rehabilitation are limited. Below is a list of options to maintain the horse's normal mental status if full-time turn out is unavailable:

- Lengthen the amount of time a horse is turned out.
- Allow the horse a stall companion like chickens, goats, or a miniature donkey.
- Increase exercise and/or ride time.
- Feed more times a day.
- Provide large portions of lower protein feeds, like grass or hay, eliminating grains. Change to a complete feed supplement or dry grain, if necessary.
- Place a mineralized salt block in the housing area.
- Purchase an equestrian-designed toy.

Chapter Four

Equine Management

Noah, the Flood

Since Noah, humans have lived on the planet with animals, using them for food, war, industry, agriculture, and pleasure. For these reasons, careful consideration should be taken when determining the purchase of a horse. Not only the emotional attachments but there are also many aspects of horse care to consider. This literary reference may help in making such an important decision: Genesis 7:19; 20 Preparation for the Flood.

"Of all living creatures, you shall bring two into the ark, one male, one female, that you may keep them alive with you. Of all kinds of birds, of all kinds of beasts, and all kinds of creeping things, two of each shall come into the ark with you to stay alive."

Equine Housing: Building, Care, and Maintenance

The first primary consideration before purchasing a horse is the housing facilities. They must be designed to protect the horse. A horse is an active, alert athlete that can often be injured due to their first defense mechanism, flight. This inherited reaction is to flee from danger, whether real or imagined.

The one major concern should be the placement of your horse facility. In recent years the number of infectious diseases has increased dramatically due to flying vectors. Avoid wet or standing water areas after a large amount of rainfall. Excavation work may be possible to improve an area. Keep ponds, pools, or washes as clean as possible and supplied with fly predators to help keep the bug population under control. Local agriculture agents will consult with you in helping to improve water conditions. Large ponds can be stocked with predaceous minnows to eat mosquitoes and larvae. Another option is hatching dragonflies (mosquito hawks) that also feed on mosquitoes. In small ponds, install a fountain or goldfish to aerate the water. Vaccinate livestock at least once a year. There is no better precaution than preventative care.

There are several items to remove from the barn area to limit flying vectors. Remove old tires as they retain water. Store grain in rodent-proof and insect-free containers; large garbage cans or plastic or metal barrels are ideal. Repair any leaky faucets, ensure good air circulation, and keep any water buckets or stock tanks clean and free from algae and food.

Clean stalls once to twice a day during high-flying vector seasons: summer and spring. Manure and waste must be kept away from the barn area in a compost pile or spreading it out to dry. Breaking the cycle of insect larvae takes ten to twenty-one days. There are numerous plants available that are natural insect repellents, such as Horsemint, Rosemary, Marigolds, Ageratum, Mosquito Plants, and Catnip.

Always repair sagging fences, broken gates, barbed wire, exposed electric wires, and protruding nails. Any fencing used to house your horses should be at least five to six feet in height and visible to the horse.

Types of Fencing and Barns

There are many common types of fencing available for horse farms and ranches. Some examples are post and rail, pipe, chain link, post and cable, vinyl, electric and woven wire. The use of barb wire for horses should be avoided; they are thin-skinned and cut very easily. If you do not own property and must house the horse at a boarding stable, the same rules apply. The list below is some common types of barns installed on horse properties.

Enclosed horse barns normally have solid walls dividing each stall, barred doors, and the stalls vary in size.

Mare motels are normally found in the western states where ventilation is necessary due to the extreme heat. These barns have a full cover with stalls underneath. Stalls also vary in size, allowing for customization by the customer.

Pole barns are completely enclosed on the outside, with one or two large doors on each end.

Paddocks are usually built for horses in the pasture. They are fully covered and can be free-standing. The size can vary according to the owner's specifications.

The most common barn floors are dirt, but some contain concrete or asphalt.   These floors must then be covered with rubber mats for sanitation reasons. Shavings are applied to the floor for cushioning and absorbency.

Arenas, Round Pens, Turn Outs

Arenas should be at least 50 x 80 feet, preferably with rounded corners.

Round pens need to be no less than fifty to sixty-five feet in diameter or seventy-five feet if riding will be done in the round pen. Rails should be at least five feet and up to seven feet in height. Solid panels will minimize injuries when working the horse in the round pen.

Turn-out pens are recommended to be at least 20 x 30 feet, which allows the horse ample room for exercising. Fencing should be five to seven feet in height as well. Using an electric fence is always an option.

Pasture

The average horse requires one to three acres of land to provide adequate forage. However, the feed may need to be supplied in winter or drought conditions. Artificial shelters should be provided if the property does not have natural shelters such as trees or other windbreaks. When exposed to rain and wind, unnecessary energy is used to maintain the horses' normal body core heat, making them susceptible to illness. During spring and fall, rapid changes in the pasture grasses increase the risk of laminitis. Precautions should be taken to remove horses for these short periods if necessary.

Feeders and Waterers

Feeders are made to hang on the fence or be placed on the ground. Either type of feeder can be found in plastic or metal. Horses should never be fed grain or hay on the ground. This causes a build-up of sand and dirt in the intestine, which leads to sand colic.

Plastic barrels can be purchased very inexpensively. Cut them into two sections to hold feed or water. Large feeders placed on the ground are a more natural position for the horse to eat, mimicking grazing. This also prevents a feeder from being placed too high on a fence.

There are many types of automatic waterers. However, daily inspection for leaks, cleanliness, and proper function of the float mechanism is a necessity. Water faucets should be placed against a building for safety.

Hay Storage

 Hay storage close to the barn is more convenient, although storing hay in the same barn with the horses is not recommended. Bailed hay can produce extreme amounts of heat in a building with inadequate ventilation and cause a fire hazard. Storing hay on pallets or poles will allow for adequate ventilation.

Feed Rooms and Tack Rooms

Feed rooms are not a necessity, but they will eliminate an escaped horse from overeating feed that is now accessible to them. Grain barrels need to be clean and rodent-proof, with tightly sealed lids. The following items are recommended for a feed room: a weigh scale, measuring scoops, bucket openers, measuring weight tapes, a storage cabinet for medicines and wound care products, a broom, a dustpan, and a refrigerator. Barn tools such as manure rakes, leaf rakes, and shovel (flat nose and pointed) need to be in a safe place, and garbage cans must have a lid.

Storing feed or grain in the tack room is not recommended. Food attracts rodents, and they can be very destructive to saddles and tack.

Saddle racks can be built on the wall or free-standing. Saddles should never be stored on the ground; leather is soft and pliable, and leaving it on the ground can change its shape. Proper placement of the saddle on the ground is upside down, or the saddle horn on the ground with the saddle in an upright position. The following items are required for the tack room: saddle racks, bridle and halter hangers, grooming box, clippers, leg protection boots, fly masks, blankets, cooling sheets, and misc. extra tack (reins, bridles, halters, lead ropes, snaps, Charlie screws, curb chains, leather straps, gullets, and latigos, along with extra saddle blankets and cinches).

Hitching Post

Hitching posts are normally made of metal and contain three posts at a height of approximately three to four feet. Corners should be rounded and smooth. There are several options for the ground under the hitching post, such as rubber mats, rough concrete, or gravel. If cross ties are preferred, the two tie ropes should be firmly anchored to the barn wall or installed upright posts when necessary.

Stall Bedding

Stall bedding can be purchased in bulk or bagged; however, bulk shavings are the most cost effective. Various types of stall bedding are available in bulk, such as pine shavings, grindings, sawdust, and sometimes a mix is available. Bagged shavings are only available in pine. Use only fresh wood products, not treated or glued materials like particleboard, old furniture, treated wood, and pallets. These materials contain nails, glue resins, and other hazardous materials dangerous to horses.

Holding bins can be built to contain bulk shavings. Bins need to have a dirt floor; concrete holds moisture, causing the shavings to mold. There should also be no solid cover. Nylon or canvas tarps are adequate cover and can be removed to dump the load of shavings. A 16 x16 stall will take approximately one yard of material to cover the floor adequately.

Stalls need to be cleaned once to twice a day, removing manure and urine spots. Start by removing the visible manure piles. Once you have located a urine spot, pull the clean shavings away, and scoop out the wet material. After you have done this, rake all the shavings away from the edges of the stall, cleaning any other exposed manure or wet shavings. Now smooth the shavings in the stall. Stalls should be stripped of all material once a month, and fresh shavings replaced. The length of time each horse spends in the stall will determine if shavings have to be replenished more than once a month. Stalled horses have higher incidences of colic, laminitis, and developing stall vices.

Before attempting to build any horse facility, please consult a licensed professional so the utmost safety can be provided for the owner and horse. When consulting a professional about building a horse facility, please remember the more natural the housing environment, the longer the life span will be for the horse. This will also minimize illnesses caused by unnatural living environments.

Chapter Five

The Question of Slaughter

"To honor the cowboy is the job bestowed to the horse by
God in heaven. From the day of birth to the silence of
death—each companion stays friends to the end."
By Anna Elizabeth

Origin of Consuming Horsemeat

In the late Paleolithic Era, wild horses were an important source of food. In pre-Christian times, horsemeat was eaten in northern Europe as a part of indigenous Germanic pagan religious ceremonies, particularly those associated with the worship of Odin. Odin is the chief god in Norse mythology. He was worshiped as the god of wisdom, war, battle, and death. The ceremonies were associated with the concept of the wild hunt, a noisy, bellowing movement across the sky, which was led by a host of slain warriors.

The taste for horsemeat began in France, a custom that dates back to the Battle of Eylau in 1807 when the surgeon-in-chief of Napoleon's Grand Army advised the starving troops to eat the flesh of the horses that died on the battlefield. The Calvary used the breastplates as cooking pans and gunpowder as a seasoning and thus founded the tradition.

Totemistic Taboo

Totemistic (tribal culture) taboo is a cultural reason for the refusal to eat horsemeat. Roman sources state that the horse goddess Epona was widely worshiped in Gaul and southern Britain; the Uffington White Horse is probable evidence of ancient horse worship. The Christian belief is horses are creations of God, sent to humans as companions in war, agriculture, society, and personal relationships or simply for sentimental reasons. In the bible, Revelations 19:1121(NIV), there are references such as:

"I saw heaven standing open and there before me was a white horse, whose rider is called Faithful and True."

Since this time, many religions have considered horsemeat taboo. For example, Jewish dietary laws forbid horsemeat because they do not have cloven hooves. In the Roman Catholic Church, the prohibition of consuming horsemeat has lingered still. Other sources of prejudice progressed from taboos to avoidance, to abhorrence. The killing of horses for human consumption is widely opposed in countries such as the USA and Britain. However, the opposition is far from unanimous; a 2007 reader's poll in the London magazine "Time Out" showed that eighty-two percent of respondents supported Gordon Ramsay's decision to serve horsemeat in his restaurants.

Countries Still Consuming Horsemeat

The high cost of living in Paris prevented many working-class citizens from buying meat such as pork or beef, so in

1866 the French government legalized the consumption of horsemeat, and the first horse butcher's shop opened. Numerous countries in the twentieth century still serve horsemeat regularly, like Austria, Belgium, Canada, Chile, China, France, Germany, Iceland, Indonesia, Italy, Japan, Kazakhstan, Malta, Mongolia, The Netherlands, Norway, Poland, Slovenia, Sweden, Switzerland, and the United Kingdom. People in the United States rarely eat horsemeat, however, during World War II, due to the low supply and high price of beef, the state of New Jersey legalized its sale. At the war's end, the state again prohibited the sale of horsemeat. Very few horsemeat-producing countries raise horses for just slaughter. Instead, they use ex-racehorses, riding horses, or unwanted horses due to abuse, lack of training, or injury.

Sometimes, horses are stolen or purchased under pretenses; the 1986 Kentucky Derby winner and 1987 Eclipse Award for Horse of the Year winner, Ferdinand, is believed to have been sent to Japan for slaughter, most likely for pet food. Horses that have been euthanized by lethal injection are not consumed, and the remains are cremated because the meat is tainted by toxins.

Process of Slaughter

In the following sections of this chapter, any horseman with love for horses will have to choke back the tears. There is an ongoing problem with horses being sold for human consumption. Nevertheless, every horse owner must be aware of the processes involved with animal slaughter. In most countries where horses are slaughtered for food, they are processed like cattle in large-scale factory abattoirs (slaughterhouses). The animals are rendered unconscious by being shot in the brain with a metal rod, using a captive bolt stunner that is pneumatically or cartridge driven. They are then killed by exsanguination ("bled out") which is done by severing the jugular vein or carotid artery while being suspended by a rear leg with a heavy chain shackle. The horses are then butchered, cut into smaller pieces for easier handling, and packaged for sale.

Polls and Legislation

In 2002, the fourteen principal countries producing horsemeat produced 700,000 tons of the product. Most people in the US are not aware of the sale of horsemeat for human consumption in other countries. Several polls were conducted in several states: in New York, 64% of people believed that the slaughter of horses for human consumption was illegal in the US, while in Indiana, 91% believed the slaughter of horses should be banned, and in Texas, 86% of voters were unaware that slaughter goes on in their state. Before 2007 three major Equine slaughterhouses were operating in the US: Dallas Crown Inc. in Kaufman, Texas; Beltex Corporation in Fort Worth, Texas; and Cavel International, Inc. in DeKalb, Illinois. All three of these companies are of Belgian ownership, although there are several others owned by French and Dutch. Forty-two million dollars' worth of horsemeat is exported each year from the US. The department of transportation has officers at the enforcement points to ensure proper transportation of the horses, but there is no jurisdiction beyond the transportation. Horses that are lame or disabled are not accepted at the plants. It is unknown what happens to these horses that are refused.

A 1998 survey was commissioned by the USDA/APHIS to determine where the welfare problems occur during transport to slaughter. They found that severe welfare problems occurred not in transport but mainly due to owner neglect or abuse before transport. Although most Americans oppose the slaughtering of horses for meat, it is important to understand the severity of the issue, which the media tends to downplay. According to the AVMA,

100,000 US horses will go to slaughter each year regardless of any legislation. The US, however, has legislation so that the horses are humanely slaughtered. But now they must travel outside the protection of national regulations and may travel without food or water for days in tightly packed trailers. The actual survival rate is unknown. The current bill introduced to the US Congress is the "American Horse Slaughter Prevention Act." This bill can be followed via the Library of Congress. Two hundred organizations oppose the ban on horse slaughter, including the American Quarter Horse Association, the American Association of Equine Practitioners, the American Veterinary Medical Association, and numerous animal agriculture groups. Many of the other agriculture groups include organizations representing traditional food animals industries such as cattle, sheep, and pork. These organizations are concerned that banning any animal from slaughter will endanger their industries. Two other arguments report that abuse would multiply if horses cannot be slaughtered, but according to UC Davis, there is no increase in cases of abuse in California, where horse slaughter is banned. The second argument is the distance horse will have to endure being sent to either Canada or Mexico.

Final Thoughts

 Any of these arguments are valid, but the fact remains horses are still being sold for human consumption while the legal issues are being settled. This makes the situation grave for the animals that are forced to endure any unregulated transport, and the one truth that cannot be argued is that death and disease are silent.

Chapter Six
Equine Nutrition

Six Main Classes of Nutrients to Survive

George Armstrong Custer and his troops may have lost the Battle of Little Big Horn because their horses were lame. Whereas Sioux chief Sitting Bull originated elsewhere, and the Indians' horses were sound. The following literary reference could refer to the historical sidelight of selenium toxicity.

"Come; let us go through the land to all the sources of water and all the streams. We may find grass and save the horses and mules so that we shall not have to slaughter any of the beasts." 1 Kings 18:5.

If any horseman ever questioned the importance of learning the art of feeding the Equine species, the previous story should answer any questions.

Like any living being on earth, Equines require six main classes of nutrients to survive: water, energy, fats, major minerals, trace minerals, and vitamins. The following list is in order or importance when feeding a horse.

Water makes up sixty-two to sixty-eight percent of the horse's body weight. Horses can go for weeks without food but only a few days without water.

An eight to ten percent loss in fluids can cause dehydration. Therefore, free access to fresh, clean water must be provided at all times. A one-thousand-pound horse will drink an average of ten to twelve gallons of water a day and more in hot weather or when consuming higher levels of salt, potassium, and magnesium. When on lush pasture or in cold weather, the amount will decrease.

Water plays a large part in digestion and producing saliva, which can be up to ten gallons a day. While exercising a horse, always provide them with water to drink. Do not let an overheated horse drink large amounts of water. Limit them to small drinks until they are cooled out. Hay or grain can be supplied after thirty to sixty minutes. Improper care of an overheated horse can lead to colic, founder, or laminitis.

Energy sources come from fat and carbohydrates. Since equids do not have a gall bladder, bile continuously flows from the liver directly into the small intestine. Fat, though necessary in the diet, is difficult for the horse to digest and utilize in large quantities.

The horses' main energy source mostly comes from carbohydrates. Soluble carbohydrates are found in nearly every feed source. Corn has the highest, then barley and oats. Forages have about six to eight percent soluble carbohydrates but can have up to thirty percent. Sudden ingestion of large amounts of starch or high-sugar feed can cause colic or laminitis.

Protein is used in all parts of the body, especially in the muscles, blood, hormones, hooves, and hair cells. Amino acids are the main building blocks for protein. The best sources can be found in alfalfa and other legumes. Most adult horses need an average of eight to ten percent protein in their daily diet. However, lactating mares require higher amounts of protein. Deficiencies in protein may result in weight loss, rough hair coat, and small offspring at birth, as well as reproduction dysfunction and depressed immune function. Excessive protein, though not harmful, will most likely just increase urine output.

 Major minerals are calcium, phosphorus, sodium, chloride, potassium, magnesium, and sulfur. Quantities are usually stated in a percentage chart on feed products.

Calcium and phosphorus are the main concern because of their profound effect on growth and development. Calcium and phosphorus are the chief constituents for healthy bones and teeth. Calcium plays a part in blood clotting and nerve impulses, while phosphorus is essential for enzyme systems and generates the transfer of energy. An imbalance in calcium and phosphorus can result in many physical abnormalities, such as deformed or brittle bones.

A recommended diet ratio is 1:1 and 2:2, and growing foals can tolerate higher ratios. The ratio of phosphorus should never be more than calcium, as over time, this can cause bone problems such as osteoporosis (a disorder that causes porous or brittle bones). Foals and young horses need a balanced diet with proper calcium and phosphorus, and trace minerals until the age of four years. Hard work will also deplete the system of sodium, potassium, and chloride, especially in hot weather. Supplementation of electrolytes can be supplied to balance their system. Sodium and chloride needs can be provided using iodized loose or block salt fed daily, no more than two ounces per day. Potassium, magnesium, and sulfur are present in adequate quantities in the hay. Therefore, supplements of these are not recommended.

Trace minerals such as copper, iodine, iron, manganese, selenium, and zinc are needed daily. However, they are only necessary in minute amounts because the exact requirements of these minerals in the body are not known yet, owing to the many interactions they perform. This is of growing concern with the increased rations of alfalfa being fed by horsemen. Fertilizing with lime will cause an increase in the molybdenum content of the forage, which may decrease the availability of copper, inducing a copper deficiency.

Trace minerals have a prominent role in building a strong skeletal system. Without a proper balance of trace minerals, bone defects start at a very early age, such as epiphysitis (a disorder in the growing end of bones) and chondrosis (degeneration of bones underlying the cartilage of joint surfaces). Barns that are seeing these disorders have benefited from a small increase of trace minerals being fed daily.

Selenium toxicity can cause ataxic (in coordinated), stiff gated hair loss, and cracked hoofs. Iron in excess or deficiency may cause the development of goiters (enlarged thyroid gland).

 Vitamins in horses are only utilized in small amounts because they cannot synthesize sufficient quantities to fulfill their daily requirements. Vitamins are only second to protein among the nutrients they are overfed the most often. Unless the horse is exposed to extreme conditions such as hard work, illness, traveling, showing, or racing, the vitamins in their daily diet of leafy green forages are more than adequate. Pasture horses do not need vitamin supplementation. However, horses under strenuous activity may require additional B vitamins. In this case, "More is not better," as severe complications can occur from vitamin toxicity.

Sources of Nutrients

Roughages (or forages) are the most common sources of nutrients. Roughages are further subdivided into legumes and grasses.

Legumes are plants that can directly absorb or "fix" (to convert atmospheric nitrogen into a useful compound) nitrogen in the air. Legumes have a taproot, whose leaves are supported by a stalk attached to the main stem. Examples of legumes are alfalfa, clovers, birds-foot trefoil, lespedeza, and vetches. Legumes are generally richer in nutrients and higher in protein and calcium.

Grasses have a fibrous root system whose leaves originate from one main stem. Examples of grasses are timothy, orchard grass, bromegrass, bluegrass, and fescue (not recommended for horses). None of the forages contain much phosphorus, and they vary in nutrients according to the stages of plant growth, soil fertility, water supply, and curing process. The following list will help you decipher the quality of forages.

Type of Plant

The higher the legume (protein) content, the higher the nutrient content.

Stage of Maturity

Earlier cut forages contain the highest content of proteins, minerals, and vitamins and improve digestibility.

Leaves contain the greatest nutrient content, so the more leaves, the better the quality.

Color is not a requirement. However, the least amount of sun bleaching, the higher the nutrient content. Sun bleaching reduces carotene (fat-soluble pigments transformed into vitamin A in the liver) and decreases palatability.

Fresh-cut forages have a good, pleasing smell to the senses. Moldy forages should be avoided at all times.

Forages should have a fine and pliable stem. Large wooded stems reduce the quality; squeezing the stem with the hand should not hurt one's palm.

Foreign material: Forages should be free of weeds, trash, dirt, and twine. These may cause problems with the horse's digestion system or even cause colic.

Grains: Processing such as rolling and cracking reduces the nutrient content. One of the most common ways to feed grains is in pre-mixed feeds. Molasses is normally added as a binder to eliminate dust and increase palatability. Caution must be used when feeding grains with molasses, as they mold easily and can be overfed. This increases the chances of colic, founder, and obesity. Molasses is sugar and will increase the energy level of the horse, promoting behavioral problems.

Concentrated or pelleted feeds should be provided in quantities no greater than one percent of the horse's body weight per day. If ratios greater than one percent are needed, it should be done with grains that have a loose mass, such as oats or barley, to help avoid impaction, colic, or founder.

Oats are the most popular grain to be fed. They have a lower digestible energy level but have a high fiber content. They form a loose mass in the stomach that is well-suited for grazing animals. Oats are also more palatable than other grains and more difficult to overfeed, reducing the risk of colic and founder. Oats can be fed whole, eliminating processing, which decreases the nutrient content.

Corn has twice the digestible energy of oats and is low in fiber. However, due to these two factors, corn can easily be overfed. This causes obesity, colic, or founder. Corn should seldom be fed alone and never feed moldy corn as it is poisonous to horses.

Barley is another popular grain, but it must also be processed to crack the seed hull and allow easier digestibility. Barley is normally found in the combination of oats and corn called "COB" or "Three Way".

Supplements

The average modern horse does not need supplements; good hay or pasture and trace minerals are adequate, and small amounts of grain are optional. However, when subjected to stress, age, reproduction, or intensive exercise such as training, showing, or ranch work, additional nutrition is necessary. Extra fat and protein, along with vitamins, are the usual supplement.

Soybean meal has an average of forty-four percent crude proteins and the proper ratio of dietary essential amino acids for Equines to digest. It is one of the most common supplements.

Vegetable and corn oils are particularly popular as well. Rice bran and flax seed is another good source, containing about twenty percent fat and fiber, and is also easily digested by the Equine.

There are thousands of commercially made supplements marketed for horses; the local feed dealer can help recommend the proper supplement to feed.

Proper Feeding of the Equine

The Equine is an herbivore in the non-ruminant family, meaning they only have one stomach. So, to ensure good digestion, equids should be allowed to forage whenever possible. The feed ration of one hundred percent forage is safe as long as legumes are no more than fifty percent of their diet. The average horse will consume one to two and a half percent of their body weight each day. This should never drop below one percent of their body weight each day. Foals will consume two to four percent of their body weight in a day until about six months of age when continuous feed is not possible. Several small feedings a day are recommended.

When supplementing grain or other concentrates, quantities must be regulated carefully. Therefore, horse feed is measured by weight, not volume. For example, one pound of oats has a different volume than one pound of corn. The mature idle horse can safely consume zero to ten percent ration of grain a day. Heavily worked horses can increase to a twenty to seventy percent ration. Concentrated or pelleted feeds should never be more than one percent of the horse's body weight per day unless instructed by a veterinarian.

Proper feed measurements must be calculated by the use of a weight tape. Place the tape around the horse's barrel, behind the elbow of the front leg. Once the horse's weight and physical condition are determined, start with one and a half percent body weight, and graduate if necessary, to maintain an ideal condition. Adjust according to exercise, age, stress, and health condition.

Salt and trace minerals are available in loose or block form. Loose salt should not be fed more than two ounces per day.

Due to the horse's digestive system, many complications occur when the horse's health is not maintained properly. Two major health issues that can increase complications when feeding the horse properly are discussed below.

Choke is in the top ten emergency calls for veterinarians. Choke is the blockage of the esophagus, and it is caused by improper chewing of dry food, treats, and cribbing (chewing wood). The horse will still be able to breathe but cannot swallow and will dehydrate quickly. A secondary condition caused by choke is aspiration pneumonia (food entering the nasal passage and going down the trachea into the lungs). Choke is a serious condition, and if left untreated, death will occur. Clinical signs are difficulty swallowing, disinterest in food, coughing, discharge from the nostrils (usually green), increased salivation, and distress. Malnourished or underweight horses are more prone to choke because they rush to eat their food.

There are some precautions you can take to decrease the risk of choke: always make sure your horses have plenty of water, change feed gradually, cut treats into smaller pieces, and place large flat stones or salt blocks in feeders to slow down the rate of ingestion. Any case of choke necessitates veterinarian care immediately.

Floating: The Equine teeth grow continuously throughout their lifetime. Over the years, the teeth wear, causing sharp edges to develop in the edges of the tooth, which interferes with mastication. When a horse cannot digest their feed properly, nutrient imbalances occur. For this reason, the horse's mouth needs to be checked on a semiannual basis. A veterinarian will perform a process known as "floating." Floating files the uneven edges on the horse's teeth, allowing them to chew properly again. Many behavioral problems other than digestion can be caused by poor dental conditions.

Chapter Seven
Horse Health

Equine Plagues

Historically, a condition known as "Lampas" was a swelling on the roof of the horse's mouth. The treatment for the supposed disease was searing the swelling with a hot iron rod, or sticking it full of holes, then filling the holes with salt. However, no amount of irritation would ever make it go away since the bulge was the thyroid gland, and trying to eliminate it was futile. Eventually, a much gentler treatment was prescribed by rubbing a mild counterirritant in the bronchiole, swelling in the throatlatch area.

In 1820, William Carver, a farrier (the profession then included horse doctoring as well as horseshoeing), itemized the six most common diseases of American horses in his book The Practical Horse Farrier.

Although, in 180 years of major medical advances, just three of the diseases - glanders, farcy, and lockjaw - have been effectively eliminated. Yet, there are many other disorders still in existence that affect the Equine daily, some being life-threatening, while others render the horse unsound or lame with a chronic condition to be treated for the remainder of their life.

Many of these diseases can be controlled by routine vaccinations and general health maintenance. Keeping a record of medical details will help in cases of emergencies, and yearly checkups should be done by the veterinarian.

First-Aid Kit

One of the priorities in any barn should be a first-aid kit. However, keep in mind that a veterinarian should be consulted before treating any sick or injured animal. The following items should be placed in a first-aid kit:

- Veterinarians' and Farrier's phone numbers.
- Paper and pencil for recording symptoms or instructions from the vet or farrier.
- Thermometer; digital is the most accurate.
- Sharp, clean scissors for first aid only.
- Flashlight and extra batteries.
- A clean bucket for washing wounds.
- A clean sponge.
- Gauze; is a better product than old cloths for cleaning the wound.
- Cotton balls for applying liquids onto the wound.
- Hypodermic syringe without the needle, used for cleaning wounds, preferred over cotton or gauze.

- ➢ Sterile saline solution or contact lens cleaner for wound cleaning.
- ➢ Latex/medical gloves.
- ➢ Clean towels and rags.
- ➢ Paper towels.
- ➢ Cotton leg wraps used for absorption.
- ➢ Gauze rolls used under bandages for wound dressing.
- ➢ Vet wrap, stable bandages or tape may be needed to keep bandages in place.
- ➢ Easy boot for hoof injuries.
- ➢ Medical grade antibacterial soap.
- ➢ Wound ointment for minor scrapes.
- ➢ Betadine soap, diluted iodine solution, or hydrogen peroxide.
- ➢ Poultice dressing, disposable diapers, or sanitary napkins to draw the moisture out of wounds.

Parasitism

Parasitism is one version of symbiosis, or living together, a phenomenon in which two phylogenetically unrelated organisms can co-exist for long periods, usually the lifetime of one of the individuals.

In the field of parasitology, the term "parasite" means eukaryotic, a pathogenic (capable of producing disease) organism. Thus, protozoan and metazoan infectious agents are classified as parasites, while bacteria and viruses are not. Fungi are not even discussed in textbooks on medical parasitology.

Parasites are known by different names according to the area of the host in which they live. The following is a list.

- Endoparasites live inside the body of the host.
- Ectoparasites live on the outside of the body.
- Epiparasites feed on other parasites; this is sometimes referred to as hyperparasitoidism.
- Parasitoids are parasites that use other organisms' tissues for their own nutritional needs until the host dies.
- Biotrophic parasites cannot survive in a dead host and therefore keep their host alive; many viruses, for example, are biotrophic because they use the host's genetic and cellular processes to multiply.

The vertebrate immune system can detect most parasites through the contact of bodily fluids. On a behavioral level, the itching sensation followed by scratching is used to fend off parasites. Below is a list of parasites explaining the effects they have on the hosts in which they survive.

Ascariasis is a human disease caused by the parasitic roundworm Ascariasis lumbricoides. Other species of the genus Ascariasis are parasitic in horses and can cause disease.

Infection occurs when contaminated fecal matter is mixed with food. The larvae hatch and burrow through the intestine into the lungs and migrate up the respiratory tract to be re-swallowed.

Oestridae is also known as the Botfly, and it is one of several families of hair flies. The larvae live as parasites within the bodies of mammals. One hundred fifty species exist in the world.

Eggs are deposited on the animal's hair, and the body heat hatches the eggs. The botfly emerges annually, in late summer or early fall. The eggs look like yellow drops of paint on the lower parts of the horse's legs. When the horse rubs their nose to scratch their legs, the eggs are transferred into the mouth. The parasite hatches, grows, and transfers to the skin, creating a thumbnail-size lump.

The eggs should be removed from the legs when noticed, using a fingernail or a single-edged razor blade if the horse will stand still safely.

Cestoda is an older name for a common intestinal virus. Cestoda, the tapeworm, lives in the digestive tract. Adult worms absorb food predigested by the host; therefore, they do not need a digestive tract or a mouth. Tapeworms are almost entirely reproductive structures. They cause several digestive problems and, left unattended, can cause intestinal blockages.

Dictyocaulus, a genus of the nematode parasite, survives in the bronchial tree of the horse. Dictyocaulus arnfeldii is the lungworm.

This parasite has a simple but interesting life span. The L1 larvae are shed in the manure or feces, then mature and become infectious as L3-stage larvae. The stage L3 larvae invade the inside of the Pilobolus sp. fungi and await fungal sporangium. When the fungi sporulate, the larvae are dispersed as much as 10 ft in a pasture.

The Dictyocaulus are most common in cattle; however, they can be found in all grazing animals. Donkeys are silent carries of this parasite and can infect your pasture or barn with the lungworm larvae.

Gasterophilus is the genus family of the botfly. These parasitic flies lay eggs around the face, lips, and nose of the horse. The eggs hatch and migrate up the nasal passage or into the stomach. Finally, the larvae are passed through the feces and burrow in the ground to pupate.

Habronema Muscae is an internal stomach parasite. Like Gasterophilus, the eggs are passed out in the feces. The larvae migrate into the mouthparts of the common house fly, where they are again passed on to the horse. It is also possible for the fly to deposit the larvae in an open wound, which can cause an ulcerated irritation called "summer sores." Another infection can occur in the eye, causing persistent conjunctivitis.

These parasites, if left unattended, can cause abscesses in the lung tissue or completely block food from passing through the intestine.

Enterobius Vermicularis is the pinworm. It lives in the small intestine and upper colon. Unlike other parasites, the pinworm usually does not enter the bloodstream or any other organs besides the intestine.

After mating, the male dies and the female migrates to the anus and deposits about 10,000 to 20,000 eggs in the perianal area. She then secretes an irritating substance on the surface. Once scratching occurs, the eggs are transferred to barn areas such as feeders and stall rails. Then they get re-ingested by the horse.

Strongyles are part of the nematode family. They are often called gastrointestinal parasites, overall, very common in horses.

Encysted Cyathostomes are a type of small strongyle that lives in the bowel wall. Large numbers of this gastrointernal parasite emerging simultaneously can cause diarrhea, especially in the winter months.

Worming the *Equine*

All Equines are burdened with parasites and therefore must have routine treatment to minimize their effects. Antihelminthics drugs expel parasitic worms (helminthes) by either killing or stunning the worm.

The major concern to horsemen is the ability of worms to develop immunity to parasitic drugs. The treatment eliminates worms whose genotype renders them susceptible; thus, worms that survive pass on their resistant genes. Always rotate wormers regularly, even if you feed daily wormers. The following is a good rotation schedule to follow.

Frequency depends on the area of the country in which the horse resides.

- ➤ Western states - worm horses quarterly.
- ➤ Eastern states - worm horses every two months.
- ➤ Types of wormer throughout the year
- ➤ April and October, worm for tapeworms.
- ➤ February and November, worm for encysted redworms.
- ➤ December, worm for bots.
- ➤ Treat all animals at the same time.
- ➤ Underdosing causes worms with low-level resistance to survive and pass on resistant genes.

The following is an example of anthelminitc drugs used to worm different parasites.

- ➤ Albendazole: Effective against threadworms, roundworms, whipworms, tapeworms, and hookworms.

- ➤ Diethylcarbamazine: Effective against wuchereria bancrofti, brugia malayi, brugia timori, tropical pulmonary eosinophilia, and loiasis.
- ➤ Mebendazole: Effective against pinworms, roundworms, and hookworms.
- ➤ Niclosamide: Effective against tapeworms.
- ➤ Ivermectin: Effective against most common intestinal worms except tapeworms.
- ➤ Thiabendazole: Effective against roundworms and hookworms.
- ➤ Pyrantel Pamoate: Effective against most nematode infections.
- ➤ Octadepsipeptides: Effective against emodepside and gastrointestinal helminthes.

One word of caution; when using Ivermectin with brand names such as Eqvalan, Zimecterin, and Rotation 1, an antibiotic, they are fermented products made of the microorganism streptomyces avermitilis. This disrupts the flow of a neuro-muscular chemical called GABA, which can be found throughout the parasite's body. Disrupting the chemical flow leads to paralysis and death of the parasite. So, in cases wherein a horse is diagnosed with sleeping sickness that causes a temporary breakdown of the protective layer of GABA around the spinal cord, these horses should not be given Ivermectin products with the brand names listed above. Parasites without GABA found in their bodies, such as tapeworms and flukes, are not affected by Ivermectin.

Moxidectin was introduced in 1997. Called Quest, it interferes with the chloride channel neurotransmission in the parasite, which disrupts a different neurological chemical than ivermectin, and allows for a broader spectrum of parasitic worming.

Two common methods of worming are used regularly. Both will adequately control re-infection: paste or daily wormers.

> ➢ Paste worming kills parasites with one single dose and is given every 8-12 weeks, depending on the area in which the horse lives.
> ➢ Continuous worming is a small, consistent dose given every day.

Paste worming eliminates large numbers of parasites at one time but is gone from the system in a few days, whereas daily wormers feed low doses of antihelminthics over long periods. However, daily wormers are not effective in horses that have large infestations of parasites. Regular worming is a necessity that must be continued throughout the horse's lifetime.

Along with the use of daily wormers or paste wormer, there are a few more steps available to limit the re-infection of worms in the horse.

> Daily cleaning of the horse's stall by removing the manure and urine spots (the average horse produces up to 15 pounds of manure and several gallons of urine a day) and continual replenishment of fresh stall bedding.
> Spreading manure and old stall bedding in an area away from the barn allows the manure to dry out, eliminating the moist breeding ground for parasites and flies.
> Install a fly system in your barn.
> Eliminate standing water, and rake and clean the barn area regularly. Keep grain in a sealed container that is clean and dry.

The most important factor when dealing with flying vectors is eliminating the smell of manure and urine. Additionally, mosquitoes are drawn to standing water.

Vaccinating the Equine

Vaccinations are an inexpensive way to ensure the horse's long-term health. Most horses should be inoculated at least twice a year, in spring and fall. Traveling horsemen should give additional boosters because of consistent contact with strange horses and new environments. Ask your local veterinarian for recommendations.

The next section of this chapter outlines the common illnesses and diseases contracted by the Equine.

Illnesses and Diseases

Vaccinated Diseases

West Nile Virus (WNV) is a mosquito-transmitted disease that affects not just horses but humans too. The virus's natural life cycle combines birds and mosquitoes. The cycle starts with infected birds traveling considerable distances in a short time. Then they are bitten by a mosquito, which then feeds on another bird, horse, human, or other mammal.

Signs of the virus can occur in five to fifteen days, and it is most prevalent from May to October. The virus established itself in the United States in 1999. Since then, it has spread throughout the world.

The most common symptoms of the disease are stumbling, incoordination, weak limbs (difficulty standing), partial paralysis, twitching, and in some cases, death. The focus of treatment is on reducing brain inflammation. In less than one-fourth of Equine cases, fever develops.

Specific medications are not available for horses at this time, but some promising advances are being made. However, veterinarians can provide supportive therapy that can save your horse's life. Most horses start showing signs of improvement in 3-5 days. Ninety percent have a full recovery within one to six months. But be advised the long-term effects of the disease are unknown at this time. Vaccinations require two doses, three to six weeks apart, followed by a single dose once a year. Once the virus is transmitted, the vaccine is of no value.

Eastern Equine Encephalitis (EEE), known as sleeping sickness or "Triple E," is a zoonotic alpha virus and arbovirus (a virus transmitted by blood-sucking arthropods, such as ticks, and fleas) present in North, Central, and South America and the Caribbean.

EEEV was first recognized in Massachusetts in 1831 when 75 horses died of encephalitic illness. Scientists first isolated the agent of EEE found in horse brains in 1933. In

1938, thirty children died from encephalitis in the northeastern USA; these outbreaks in children coincided with outbreaks in horses in the region. Mosquitoes, ticks, lice, and mites transmit the disease. Symptoms occur one to three weeks after infection. Fever can reach up to one hundred and six degrees, and complete paralysis and death occur in two to four days. The mortality rate is seventy to ninety percent in horses.

EEE can be prevented by vaccination, usually given in conjunction with WEE, VEE, and tetanus. Horses with "sleeping sickness" should not be given Ivermectin due to the disruption of the flow of (GABA) in the central nervous system.

African Horse Sickness (AHS) is highly infectious and very deadly. It commonly affects horses, donkeys, mules, and zebras. Although AHS is not directly contagious, it is known to be spread by insect vectors. Warm, humid climates constitute "epidemic areas." However, larvae do not carry the virus, and long, cold winters are sufficient to break epidemics in "non-epidemic areas."

Horses are the most compatible host, with close to a ninety-percent mortality rate for those infected. As devastating as this disease is, there is currently no treatment for AHS.

Animals affected by this disease are usually euthanized. Vaccinations for AHS will prevent the infection of other horses.

Strangles (Equine distemper) is an upper respiratory tract infection. A non-lethal disease, strangles is endemic to domesticated horses.

Symptoms include fever, nasal discharge, pus, and swollen or enlarged mandibular lymph nodes around the neck and face. Complications, called bastard strangles, are possible (strangles which has spread to other areas of the body).

The average length of the infection is twenty-three days. This infection is highly contagious, and affected horses should be isolated for about six weeks to ensure that the disease is not still incubating. In some cases, the mandibular lymph may need to be lanced, although they can rupture on their own. Vaccinations are available for this disease.

Horse Flu (Equine influenza) is endemic to horses, and it was isolated in 1956. This is one of many types of viruses that infect a horse's heart muscle. The usual symptoms include fever, a dry hacking cough, a runny nose, and a reluctance to eat or drink. Recovery takes about two to three weeks.

This is one of the most common and least severe diseases, with a nearly one hundred percent infection rate in unvaccinated horses. Since the disease is so common and persistent, vaccinations are recommended every six months.

Equine Herpes Virus 1 (EHV -1) is from the virus family Herpesviridae that causes a miscarriage in horses. The initial spread of the virus is by a newly introduced horse through direct or indirect contact; infection can lead to seventy percent of abortions or prenatal infection. Abortions occur in the last four months of gestation. Prenatal (around the time of birth) infection can lead to pneumonia and death. Encephalitis can occur in infected animals, leading to ataxia (loss of coordination in extremities), paralysis, and death.

Great discoveries have been made in identifying different mutations of a single virus during an outbreak. This virus has two types of vaccines: one is killed, and one is modified live.

Pregnant mares are vaccinated with the killed virus at five, seven, and nine months of gestation. Foals at the age of three months are vaccinated with modified live, and a booster should be given at 4 months and then once a year during their life span.

Equine Herpes Virus 4 (EHV-4) causes rhinopneumonitis in horses. EHV-4 is the source of the highest rate of respiratory infection in foals. Like other herpes viruses, EVH-4 causes a lifelong latent (apparent or present, but not visible) infection in affected animals. Most horses affected are foals over two months old, weanlings, and yearlings.

Recovery takes one to three weeks, but death can occur when animals are stressed due to overcrowding. Infected foals need to be placed in a clean, dry stall away from other horses during their recovery.   Vaccinations are available.

Potomac Horse Fever (PHF) is a febrile (fever) disease affecting only horses. Potomac Fever was first seen in areas around the Potomac River in Washington, D.C., in the 1980s. The causative agent is neorickettsia risticii, an intracellular bacterium. Symptoms can occur quickly and include high fever, mild colic-like symptoms, profuse watery diarrhea, edema because of protein imbalances, acute laminitis and/or founder. Death usually occurs from

severe laminitis and founder. However, PHF responds well
to tetracycline antibiotics, providing the laminitis or
founder is not too severe. A vaccine is available but does
not cover all strains of bacteria, so veterinarians have
recommended farm management to prevent the disease.

The vector is believed to be a trematode (parasitic flatworm
with suckers on the outside) fluke. The life cycle takes it
through freshwater snails and back into the water, where
the larvae are eaten by several aquatic insects. The
infection comes through accidental ingestion of infected
adult insects. The natural history and complete life cycle
are not yet known. PHF is not spread directly from horse
to horse.

The following management recommendations are advised:
maintaining riparian barriers along bodies of water
encourages aquatic insects to stay near their places of
origin. Turning off outside lights will prevent insects from
being attracted. Keeping water buckets and feed areas clean
will reduce the chance a horse will accidentally ingest
infected insects.

The Following Diseases Have No Vaccines Available

Equine Infectious Anemia (EIA) is known as swamp fever. Transmission is usually by blood-sucking insects. The virus survives up to 4 hours in the carrier. Mares can transmit to a foal via the placenta.

This disease is highly contagious, and there is no vaccine at this time. The virus mutates frequently, which makes it difficult to produce an effective one.

There are three forms of EIA, each with its symptoms.

Acute EIA: High fever, anemia, weakness, swelling of the lower abdomen and legs, weak pulse, and irregular heartbeat, causing the horse to die suddenly.

Sub-Acute EIA: Recurrent fever, weight loss, enlarged spleen, anemia, and swelling in the lower chest, abdominal wall, penile sheath, scrotum, and legs.

Chronic EIA: Tires easily from work, may have recurrent fever and anemia, and may develop acute symptoms.

A horse may not appear to have any symptoms of the disease but test positive for EIA antibodies. Most horses diagnosed EIA positive do not usually show any sign of the sickness or disease; however, they can still transmit the disease to other horses. A recent study in Brazil showed that horses living in the wild were thirty percent more likely to be chronically infected with EIA and living normal lives. In the 1970s, Dr. Leroy Coggins developed a test for EIA.

Federal authorities strongly enforce the rules for any horse that tests positive for EIA, because of the limited scientific effects this disease has on the world's Equine industry. In the USA, there is no current eradication program due to the low rate of incidence. Most states and other countries require a negative Coggins test.

There are several options for horsemen whose Equine tests positive for EIA: sending the horse to a recognized research facility, branding the horse and quarantining them at least 200 yards from other horses for the remainder of its life, or euthanasia (putting the horse to sleep).

Equine Protozoal Myeloencephalitis (EPM) is a protozoal infection of the central nervous system that was discovered in the 1960s by Dr. Jim Rooney. At that time, the disease was considered rare; however, since then numerous cases have been reported. Research has labeled the opossum as the carrier host. This parasite, however, needs two hosts to survive: a definitive and an intermediate host. In the laboratory, the raccoon, cat, armadillo, skunks, and sea otter are the intermediate hosts. The opossum is the definitive host. The horse is labeled a dead host, meaning EPM cannot be contracted from one horse to another.

Horses commonly contract the disease by grazing or drinking in areas where opossums have defecated recently. Therefore, the disease is not contagious. The difficulty with this diagnosis is that symptoms can mimic almost any other neurologic disorder, and this causes a wide array of problems can occur. The most common signs include asymmetric (not identical on both sides) coordination (ataxia), weakness, spasticity, and back pain, which can be severe. The actual method by which the sarcocystis neurona infects the horse is unknown.

Research has shown it prefers infecting the leukocytes (white blood cells), enabling it to cross the blood-brain barrier. If caught soon enough, the disease can be cured; antiprotozoal drugs are preferred. The most common is trimethoprim-sulfamethoxazole, an antimicrobial, along with anti-inflammatory medication. Therapy is recommended, along with injections of vitamin E and folic acid. The prognosis is variable. About sixty- percent respond to therapy, while others have sustained tissue damage too severe to reverse and leave undesirable effects.

The symptoms can take between two weeks to two years to emerge. The best recommendation is to control contact between opossums and horses. Start with keeping all food covered and out of reach of an opossum, especially cat food.

EPM is now controlled by a new vaccination released that attacks the parasite. The vaccine is only conditionally approved by the USDA until an efficiency test is available.

Cushing's syndrome was discovered in the 1930s by Harvey Cushing, an endocrinologist. Cushing's is a disease that specifically refers to a tumor on the pituitary gland, which aberrantly stimulates an excessive release of cortisol from the adrenal gland. This is characterized by abnormal fat deposition, a syndrome that leads to weight loss, polyuria, or polydipsia which causes laminitis.

Polydipsia is a condition where the patient consumes large amounts of water, causing dehydration due to excessive urination. If prolonged, this condition will cause kidney failure.

Polyuria is frequent urination

Peripheral Cushing's disease, or more properly, Equine Syndrome X (EMS), which believed to play a major role in the onset of laminitis. The primary factor here is insulin resistance. Other contributing factors may include cortisol metabolism (the corticosteroid hormone), which is produced by the adrenal cortex and is known as the "stress hormone."

Adipocyte turnover is cells that primarily specialize in storing energy as fat. EMS is similar to type II diabetes in humans, where the action of insulin is impaired. This syndrome can mimic Cushing's disease but with a normal pituitary-adrenal axis.

EMS is implicated in the development of laminitis due to compensated (counterbalance or offset) insulin resistance, which is essential for physiological and health-sustaining issues. Therefore, only when the compensatory mechanism fails does laminitis ensue. This may support the supposition that EMS is an evolved survival trait. Symptoms will be the same in a horse that is insulin resistant as a horse with EMS. They become easily obese and may have abnormal fat deposits in the neck, shoulders, loin, above the head and eyes, and tail. They generally tend to be lethargic.

Treatment includes managing the horse's adipocyte level (fat cells) by controlling weight through dietary restriction and exercise. Clinical improvement has been reported with just five to ten percent weight loss. Peripheral Cushing's disease is a condition that cannot be cured but can be managed with a success rate.

Mare Reproductive Loss Syndrome (MRLS) was first identified in April 2001 by Dr. Thomas Riddle. Some consider this disease to be a modern Equine plague. There were at least 600 fetal miscarriages in three weeks.

During the spring of 2001, Kentucky experienced an unusually heavy infestation of caterpillars. The exact mechanism by which the caterpillars caused MRLS is unknown, but it cost the racing industry an estimated 500 million dollars.

The Following Syndromes are Genetic Disorders

Hyperkalemic Periodic Paralysis (HYPP), known as Impressive syndrome (AQHA Quarter Horse stallion), is an inherited autosomal (any chromosome other than sex) dominant disorder. It affects sodium channels in muscle cells and the ability to regulate potassium levels in the blood. This is most common in horses but also affects humans. Characteristics include muscle twitching, weakness, and paralysis.

HYPP is a dominant genetic disorder. Therefore, heterozygote (having a dissimilar pair of genes for any hereditary characteristic) bred to genotypic (a single trait or set of traits, parent to offspring) normal horses will likely reproduce affected offspring fifty percent of the time. The treatment of effected horses will fluctuate with each animal. Episodes of HYPP can come on suddenly, and the horse may lose control of its body. Therefore, only experienced riders should ride these affected horses, even if the horse is currently undergoing treatment.

There were 55,000 living descendants of Impressive (AQHA Quarter Horse stallion) in 2003. Many registration associations like AQHA now mandate testing for HYPP and will no longer register horses that test positive for this disease.

In 1994, researchers were able to locate the genetic mutation and developed a blood test. Using the blood test, horses can be identified as H/H, meaning they have the mutation, and it is homozygous. In this case, the horse always passes on the disease. N/H means they have the mutation, and it is heterozygous. Here, the horse is affected to a lesser degree and will pass on the gene fifty percent of the time. N/N means they do not have the mutation and cannot pass it on, even if they are descendants of Impressive. This is a genetic mutation and cannot be cured, but treatment is available.

Lethal White Syndrome (LWS) is becoming a common genetic disorder primarily associated with the American Paint Horse. Foals are born nearly all white and have a non-functioning colon. There is no treatment or cure for LWS, and most foals die within two weeks. Be cautious: not all foals born white have LWS syndrome. The foal may just be born ill and need treatment.

LWS was discovered in 1982 when two overoes (irregular white patches, usually in a horizontal pattern) paint horses produced the condition called overo Lethal White Syndrome. Not all overos carry the LWS gene, but it is most common in paint horses.

Researchers have been able to develop a reliable DNA test for LWS. However, the syndrome is so widespread in the paint horse breed, and it has become difficult for breeds to avoid the horses carrying the gene. LWS is present in heterozygous (having dissimilar pairs of genes) form, not homozygous (parts of all the same kind), and can be found in any color horse or breed. The best safety measure is to have your mare and stallion DNA tested.

The Following List is Lymphatic Diseases

The lymphatic system is a complex network that controls the majority of the immune system. There are three interrelated systems that the lymphatic system controls: (1) removal of excess fluids from body tissue, (2) absorption of fatty acids and subsequently transport fat as chyle to the circular system, and (3) produce immune cells such as lymphocytes and monocytes.

Equine Lymphangitis is an inflammation or swelling of a limb resulting from impairment of the lymphatic system. It occurs from a secondary bacterial infection, even when the test cultures are negative. The infection will cause extreme swelling of a limb, usually a hind limb; the leg may swell to twice or three times its normal size.

Horses may not necessarily have a fever, but ridding the body of infection is of utmost importance, or the disease may recur. Controlling the swelling can be frustrating and difficult to manage, but the longer the infection lasts, the more permanent the damage. There are many forms of treatments, both herbal and homeopathic.

Epizootic Lymphangitis is a highly contagious disease among horses caused by the fungus Histoplasma farciminosum. This disease is similar to glanders but without the presence of the Histoplasma organism found in the pus of an abscess. Skin eruptions such as in the lymph nodes in the skin stand out, and nodules suppurate (discharge), forming abscesses and thick yellow pus. The ulcers heal with difficulty, even under treatment. Controlling lymphangitis is done through the elimination of the infection.

The Following List is Respiratory Illnesses

Recurrent Airway Obstruction (RAO), also known as "broken wind" in humans, is COPD. This is a chronic condition in horses involving allergic bronchitis characterized by wheezing, coughing, and labored breathing.

Allergens are typically from dust and mold spores and aspergillus ssp, which is common in horses fed hay or bedded on straw. Endotoxins from organisms in the bedding and feed may also play a role.

This condition is common in the Northern Hemisphere and rare in the Southern states, most likely due to horses being stalled over the winter months. Similar conditions apply to summer-pastured horses that develop allergens derived from fodder and pasture. If a rider notices these symptoms in their horse, they should consult a veterinarian immediately for treatment and recommendations for managing this condition.

Common Eye Disorders

Cataphract is an opacity that develops in the crystalline lens of the eye or its envelope. Early development of age-related cataracts causes myopia (near-sightedness) and a gradual yellowing and opacification of the lens, which may reduce the perception of blue colors. With time the cataract cortex liquefies to form a milky white fluid called a Morgagnian Cataract. This may cause severe inflammation and rupture. Untreated cataracts can lead to blindness and phacomorphic glaucoma.

Cataphract comes from the Greek word kataphraktos, meaning behind barriers or behind a fence. Historically, the cataphract was a heavily armed or armored cavalryman. This transformed into the name for the eye disorder. In ancient times spontaneous posterior dislocations were regarded as a blessing from the heavens because the dislocation restored some perception of light in the affected bilateral (two or both sides) patients.

 Glaucoma is increased pressure in the eye caused by a blockage or clogs which keep the eye from draining. Increased eye pressure can cause the eye to stretch and enlarge.

Glaucoma is classified into two categories:

> ➤ Primary glaucoma is an inherited condition, usually starting in one eye and graduating to both eyes leading to blindness.

> ➤ Secondary glaucoma occurs when another eye disease, such as uveitis, the pigmented vascular tunic of the eye, causes a decrease in fluid drainage, inflaming the eye (uveitis). This, in turn, can cause advanced cataracts, cancer of the eye, subluxation or luxation (displaced or malpositioned lens within the eye, caused by ocular trauma), or chronic retinal detachment.

Pressure damage to the optic nerve and decreased blood flow to the retina can cause blindness in just hours. Increased intraocular pressure in animals is higher than in humans and extremely painful. Therefore, precautions should be taken; animals are unable to communicate vocally when they are in pain. Vision loss in the one eye is inevitable, but most animals can compensate with the other eye. Horses, however, rely heavily on their eyesight and may become very skittish while they adjust to the change. A veterinarian can recommend options.

Uveitis (ERU) is an inflammation of the middle layer of the eye (uvae). Urgent treatment is necessary to control the inflammation. In some cases, uveitis causes secondary glaucoma.

There is a theory that for secondary glaucoma to occur, antibodies are developed in the body to fight infectious organisms like leptospirosis (bacterial infection) and onchocerciasis (parasitic infection).

Genetics plays a particularly important role in certain breeds that seem to be affected more often. ERU requires life-long treatment and eventually may result in removal of the eye since each attack causes more damage to the eye. Such damage becomes very painful.

Keratitis is an inflammation of the cornea that has multiple causes, the first being a present or previous herpes simplex virus infection. The secondary is an upper respiratory infection.

Symptoms include redness, sensitivity to light and pain, and blurred vision. Remember, animals are unable to communicate verbally, so it's important to observe a horse's normal habits.

Conjunctivitis (pink eye) is an inflammation of the conjunctiva (the outermost layer of the eye and the inner eyelid). This is normally caused by an allergic reaction or an infection, either bacterial or viral.

Bacterial conjunctivitis is normally caused by pyogenic bacteria such as staphylococcus or streptococcus (the patient's skin or respiratory flora). Others are due to environmental factors such as insects or contact with infected horses. Treatment includes eye drops or ointments given for approximately five days until symptoms dissipate.

Viral conjunctivitis is normally caused by contact with a variety of contagious viruses, including many that cause the common cold, so it is often associated with upper respiratory tract symptoms. Viral conjunctivitis requires immediate medical attention. The appropriate treatment depends on the cause of the problem.

This disease mostly occurs during the rainy season and winter months. The increased dampness causes additional spores to spread. The utmost care must be taken not to transfer the infection from one animal to another or yourself. Pink eye is highly contagious. For the best results, contact the veterinarian immediately.

The Following Are Different Forms of Horse Colic

Colic is the oldest known disorder of horses, as stated by Columella in the first century after Christ. At that time, the mortality rate among the sixty thousand horses in the Prussian Army was twelve percent from 1880-1900. Most of these deaths were due to parasites that induced colic.

Colic means abdominal pain. However, that is a clinical (an observation) sign rather than a diagnosis (determined by medical exam). The foremost problem with colic is the difficulty in determining the severity of the condition. Therefore, all colic cases should be taken seriously and require immediate attention by a veterinarian. For best results, treatment must be provided promptly.

Once the horse has been clinically diagnosed with colic, immediately call the veterinarian. Then follow the proceeding instructions:

➢ Take all food away from the horse.

➢ Walk him; this will help divert their attention from the pain. However, note that walking may exhaust the horse, and some cases of colic can become worsened. Ask the veterinarian for their recommendations.

Colicky horses will roll to help alleviate the abdominal pain. Be very cautious, as the horse will have no regard for the handler's safety at this time. If they cannot be stopped from rolling, place them in an area in which they will not injure themselves, then wait for the veterinarian. It is imperative the horse is not left alone.

Colic surgery is very expensive and the major cause of premature death among domestic horses. The next section explains the different types of colic in the Equine.

Pelvic Flexure Impaction is when food material becomes impacted at the pelvic flexure of the left colon, which makes a one hundred and eighty-degree turn and narrows considerably. Most cases develop from horses eating large amounts of foodstuff, and/or when they have dental issues such as spurs on the edges of the teeth or impacted teeth. Either of these causes improper mastication by the horse.

Spasmodic Colic means increased peristaltic contractions. As a result of these contractions, the horse builds up gases in the intestine, causing pain. Normally this is caused by the animal eating too much fresh grass in a short period. For example, in the fall, when the nights start to cool, the horses have not grown their winter coats, and they eat excessively to keep warm. Under such conditions, their bodies cannot digest the food quickly enough, resulting in spasmodic colic.

The Ileal (the last part of the small intestine that ends in the cecum) is affected by Impaction Colic. This is when an impaction is caused by an obstruction of ingesta frequently caused by ascarids (roundworms) or tapeworms (crestodas), or other common parasites.

Sand Colic is the condition that occurs when horses graze on sand or dirt, either in stalls or pastures that have been grazed heavily. The dirt and sand accumulate in the intestine and trigger irritation of the bowel lining, resulting in diarrhea. The weight and abrasion of the sand and dirt cause the bowel to become inflamed, minimizing motility and even causing peritonitis (partial or complete paralysis of the musculature of the bowel wall). This slows or blocks the flow of intestinal ingesta and gases.

The historical treatment used laxatives like oils or psyllium husks. However, doctors now prefer to treat horses with symbiotic (the living together of two dissimilar organisms), prebiotic (in advance of life or living beings), and psyllium combinations. Nevertheless, some cases will need surgery because horses with sand or dirt impaction are predisposed to Salmonella infection.

Horses should be prevented from eating or grazing on heavily tracked areas. Prophylactic (preventative) treatments for colic are available and have very impressive results if used properly and consistently. Consult a professional to recommend the proper course of action because different areas of the US require alternate courses to limit colic cases in horses.

Enteroliths are round balls of mineral deposits that form around foreign material ingested by the horse. When the Enterolith moves from the original site, it can obstruct the intestine and cause colic. Most obstructions of this type require surgery. Horses that are fed high rations of alfalfa hay or eat in sandy soil are predisposed to sand colic.

Parasitic Colic occurs when a large number of worms die and block the intestine, colon, or cecum. Many of these cases also require surgery.

Displacement Colic is the movement of the intestine to an alternate position. This form of colic includes intestinal twits. Surgery may be necessary, although medical advancements have allowed many horses to recover with proper exercise and medications. Caution: displacement colic is extremely painful and requires immediate attention by a veterinarian.

Other problems or diseases can mimic signs of colic. Therefore, it is imperative for a horseman to be aware of the horse's normal behavior and understand the signs of colic. Any irregularity in the horse's normal behavior should be diagnosed by a veterinarian.

Some mares will experience colic after foaling, and this is not abnormal if it is mild and does not continue for more than 20 minutes. Some mares will experience colic before foaling; in these situations, consult a veterinarian immediately.

The following list is some common signs of colic in the Equine.

> - Reluctance to eat.
> - May look at their sides and even nip at them.
> - Aggressive kicking or pawing at the abdomen.

- No fresh bowel movements in the stall.
- The horse may become constipated; however, this could be a sign of a more severe symptom of colic.
- Rolling and trashing around violently, pawing at the ground, and getting up and down repeatedly in a short period.
- Excessive sweating.
- Cool extremities like the lips or inside of the mouth.

Caution: A horse's temperature usually will not increase with colic, and the horse may have cool extremities such as the lips and legs. Check for fever: normal is one hundred and one degrees. If anything above normal, call for help immediately, as this may indicate a more serious problem.

Horsemen can take some simple precautions to reduce the incidence of colic. For example;

- Keep all feed storage bins either behind closed doors or sealed in containers. This is in the event a horse gets loose from the stall, pasture, or turn out. Closed, sealed containers eliminate the chance a horse might gorge themselves on grain or high protein feeds, causing colic or founder. Grains without molasses limit the chance of overfeeding a horse.

- ➢ Do not allow the horses to consume any spoiled grains, hay, stagnant water, or other contaminated sustenance.
- ➢ Do not feed horses on the ground. Place feed in feeders designed for an Equine.
- ➢ Feed horses on a regular schedule, and be sure to graduate any feed changes. Provide additional meals a day with smaller portions, mimicking a more natural living environment.
- ➢ Worm the horses consistently, using a yearly calendar.

The Following Are Horse Hoof Disorders and Syndromes

Laminitis and Founder

Laminitis and founder have been misunderstood for years. Technically, founder means any chronic change in the structure of the foot.   Laminitis is a disease of the sensitive laminae of a horse's foot.

On the top surface of the coffin bone (distal third phalanx) are the sensitive laminae of the Equine foot. The inflammation of the laminae is no longer thought to be the key mechanism of the disease process. Two possible sources are responsible for the consequences of this disease.

Sinking results in the cataclysmic failure of the interdigitation between the sensitive and insensitive laminae around the hoof. This allows the entire bony column of the PIII bone to sink to the bottom of the hoof capsule, developing into what is called founder (a nautical term meaning to sink).

Rotation occurs when the damage is less severe; however, it is mainly in the toe area. One possible source is the deep flexor tendon pulling the dorsal face of the coffin bone away from the hoof wall. This is preceded by the body weight continuing to force the rotation of the coffin bone, resulting in a misalignment between PII and PIII. In severe cases, the rotation causes the PIII bone to be pushed through the hoof sole and become exposed.

Not all horses with laminitis will founder, but horses that founder will first experience laminitis. In all laminitis cases, a clear distinction must be determined to verify the location of the onset and to identify whether it's an acute or chronic situation.

A chronic situation can be stable or unstable. Determining the difference between acute, chronic, stable, and unstable is of vital importance when choosing a treatment protocol.

Laminitis

Laminitis can be mechanical (external influences), systemic (metabolic disturbance), unilateral (one foot), or bilateral (two feet), or may occur in all four feet.

Systemic Laminitis is a metabolic disturbance within the horse, which results in the dysfunction of the epidermal and dermal laminae that attach the coffin bone to the hoof wall. This dysfunction allows the deep flexor tendon and the coffin bone to pull the bone away from the hoof wall instead of flexing the foot. Once the coffin bone is pulled away from the hoof wall, the remaining laminae will tear. This increases the risk of abscesses within the hoof capsule.

This results in severe pain for the horse. In some cases, the laminae can form a wedge between the front of the hoof wall and the coffin bone, preventing proper re-attachment of the laminae. Some situations permit this wedge to be surgically removed.

Mechanical Laminitis does not start with laminitis or rotation. Rather, the wall of the hoof is pulled away from the bone as a result of external influences. Mechanical founder occurs when a horse habitually paws, is ridden or driven on hard surfaces continuously, or loses laminar function because of injury or pathologies affecting the wall.

The Following Are Causes of Laminitis

Any rotation of the PIII bone must be addressed immediately. Re-establishing proper alignment is essential for long-term results because once rotation has occurred, it inhibits the possibility of a one hundred percent correction. To ensure proper recovery, stabilization of the coffin bone can be accomplished by several treatments, such as corrective trimming and/or proper shoeing, and medications may be an option to assist in the recovery. The next section is a list of the possible causes of the onset of laminitis.

Carbohydrate overload is one of the most common causes of laminitis. It develops from excess accumulation of non-structural carbohydrates, such as sugars, starch, or fructan being ingested by the horse. Current theory suggests that the accumulation of non-structural carbohydrates in the foregut is unable to digest all the excess and then moves on to the hindgut and ferments in the cecum. The presence of the fermenting carbohydrate in the cecum causes the proliferation of lactic acid bacteria and an increase in acidity. This process kills beneficial bacteria that ferment fiber. The endotoxins and exotoxins are then absorbed into the bloodstream due to the increased gut permeability caused by irritation of the gut lining due to increased acidity. The endotoxaemia results in impaired circulation, particularly in the feet, causing the development of laminitis.

Hard ground increases the concussion upon the horse's feet; therefore, the harder the work, the greater the risk of laminitis. Avoid long periods of exercise on surfaces such as concrete, blacktop, or hard dirt roads.

Nitrogen Compound Overload is when herbivores ingest high levels of potentially toxic non-protein nitrogen (NPN) compounds in their forage, such as lush spring grass grown on artificial nitrogen fertilizer used in lowland pastures. This can cause the natural metabolic processes to be overloaded, resulting in a liver disturbance and toxic imbalance. Many weeds eaten by horses are nitrate accumulators. Clover is also a nitrate collector. These overloads of nitrogen can cause laminitis.

Insulin Resistance in the horse can cause laminitis; see Equine Metabolic Syndrome (EMS), which is an insulin resistance syndrome. Insulin-resistant horses become very obese quickly, even when starved down. Insulin resistance may be a survival mechanism for Equines that live in harsh environments with sparse grass. The old saying goes, "lay down the fat when conditions are good."

The mechanism by which laminitis occurs is not fully understood yet, but these horses and ponies react to very small elevations of sugar and starch in their diet. Slow adaption to pasture is not effective, as the laminitis seems to be caused by microbial populations. These horses must be removed from pasture completely and fed hay not to be higher than eleven percent, NSC (Nonstructural carbohydrates) sugar, starch, and fructan. Removing excess carbohydrates is essential for any horse with laminitis associated with obesity or abnormal fat deposits.

Symptoms of laminitis are very easy to ascertain, but diagnosis and treatment of the exact cause are essential for recovery. Apparent signs are as follows:

The horse will attempt to decrease the load on their affected feet by rocking backward on their hind legs, which draws its hind legs under their body, easing the pressure on the toe of the front foot or feet.

Lying down whenever possible due to the extreme pain produced by the laminitis. Standing can be extremely difficult.

> ➤ Increased temperature in the hoof wall and sole.
> ➤ Anxiety.
> ➤ Visible trembling.
> ➤ Sweating.

Treatment must be immediate to ensure the horse's health. The longer laminitis is left unattended, the more damage will be done.

Lameness in one front or back leg naturally causes the horse to favor the injured leg, applying additional pressure on the sound foot. The uneven weight distribution for prolonged periods can cause founder. This may have been the cause of laminitis in Kentucky Derby winner Barbaro in 2007, which forced his owners to end his life.

Navicular Disease or Syndrome

Navicular disease is a soundness problem; therefore, it is properly termed a "syndrome," not a disease. Navicular syndrome is an inflammation or degeneration of the navicular bone and its surrounding tissues.

The navicular bone is one of the tarsal bones found in the foot. The name derives from the bone's resemblance to a small boat: the deep concave proximal aticular surface (the hollowed inward surface situated toward the point of origin).

Behind the coffin bone and under the small pastern bone lies the navicular bone. Down the back of the cannon bone runs the deep flexor tendon (DDF), which covers the soft tissue under the navicular bone before attaching to the coffin bone.

When the tendon flexes, the coffin joint and the navicular bone act as a fulcrum that the DDF tendon runs over. Supported on all four sides by ligaments, the navicular bone attaches directly to the coffin bone. These bones are protected by cartilage, and in turn, the DDF is protected by the navicular bursa (a small sac that protects the DDF and the navicular bone from abrasion as the tendon slides over the area).

The Foundation Effects of Navicular Syndrome

Even though there is no single cause of navicular syndrome, there are two basic theories about the origin - compression, and tension - explained in the next section.

Compression is a biochemical change in the hoof. This has led veterinarians to believe that the degeneration of the navicular bone is caused by the common disease osteoarthritis.

When Pedal P3 is exposed to repeated compression from the DDF and the small pastern bone, degeneration starts in the cartilage and can eventually lead to cartilage erosion. The erosion of the underside of the bone exposes the bone, which can instigate navicular bursitis (inflammation of the navicular bone).

Without consistent treatment, the constant compression increases the bone density directly under the cartilage surface, making it brittle and likely to break.

Tension is believed by experts to start when excess strain is placed on the ligaments, leading to the degeneration process.

Tension causes strain and inflammation, and this inflammation of the impaired ligament can decrease the blood flow to and from the navicular bone. Continuous excess strain can thicken the ligament and permanently reduce blood flow to the navicular bone. Since veins are more likely to be compressed than arteries, blood flow out of the foot will decrease. This increase in pressure in the hoof and decreased blood supply will cause mineral absorption from the center of the navicular bone, making it brittle.

One major contributing factor allows the initial development: conformation defects in the horse. These certain conformation faults include upright pasterns, small feet, narrow upright feet, and long toes with low heels.

> ➢ The low heel conformation places constant stress on the navicular bone, even as the horse is standing.
> ➢ The upright feet increase concussion, especially in the heel region of the hoof, where the navicular bone is located.
> ➢ Poor hoof shape is normally inherited; although poor shoeing and trimming can also contribute.

Navicular syndrome is not curable and will shorten the horse's life expectancy. Although corrective shoeing, exercise, drugs, and even surgery are available, prevention is the best method. Ask the veterinarian and farrier for their recommendations.

The Following Are Common Hoof Injuries

Important: Do not remove a foreign object found in a foot until the farrier and/or veterinarian arrives. They will determine the location and depth of the puncture.

Puncture Wounds in the foot are common in horses, and the clinical sign is lameness. The simplest puncture wound just penetrates the sole, causing a small hole and abscess, and most of the time, the foreign body does not remain in the foot, making the diagnosis difficult. A sterile probe must be inserted in the foot, which will determine the direction and depth of the puncture. If the puncture wound has penetrated the coffin bone, an x-ray must be done to determine the extent of damage. The veterinarian and farrier will consult on the treatment necessary. The recommended treatment must be followed exactly to ensure a full recovery.

Gravel is a common term used to describe drainage from the coronary band from an infection that abscessed and has worked its way up the hoof.

Gravel may be a secondary occurrence caused by "seedy toe." The possibility for treatment and recovery is excellent unless the infection causes laminitis.

Thrush is a degenerative condition of the frog caused by unsanitary conditions and extreme moisture. A physical examination of the frog will determine the extent of infection.

Signs of thrush are a foul smell when cleaning the foot and a blackening of the frog. In severe cases, large portions of the frog can fall off or cause limb swelling.

Treatment consists of improving housing conditions, removal of dead frog tissue, and application of a topical antiseptic like bleach or thrush treatment antiseptics. Prognosis is good as long as housing conditions improve.

Hoof Wall Cracks usually originate at the weight-bearing surface of the wall. Coronary band defects may produce hoof wall cracks that progress down the wall, known as toe cracks, quarter cracks, or heel cracks.

➢ The location and length of the crack will determine the correct treatment.
➢ For small cracks, a bar shoe is usually all that is necessary to stabilize the foot and prevent further progression.

> With large cracks, synthetic materials can be used to stabilize the crack, along with toe clips attached to each side of the bar shoe for additional support.

> Coronary cracks that are caused by an injury may require surgical repair of the coronary band.

> Treatment to the horse's hoof should be advised by the veterinarian and farrier.

The Following Are Common Skin Disorders

Skin is the outer covering of the body and the primary interface between the body and the environment. Skin is composed of three major layers: the epidermis, dermis, and sub cutis. Skin is the thermo regulator of heat, cold, pain, and touch, while the mane, tail, and body hair provide effective protection against insects.

The Equine has highly sensitive skin that contains numerous sensory endings, including nerve connections in the hair follicles and on the tactile hairs of the muzzle. The following list is some of the most common skin disorders.

Dew Poisoning is weeping patches with thick scabs embedded in the hair, primarily on the lower legs and muzzle. It is caused by certain plants in the pasture or turn out. Wash with warm water and soap, then treat with corticosteroids or zinc oxide.

Lice are tiny parasitic insects that live in the hair coat of horses or other mammals. Lice are species-specific, meaning that bird lice generally won't live on people or dogs, and horse lice don't typically infect people. You're not likely to get lice from your horse or pass them on to your cat. Lice infestations can be but are not necessarily an indication of poor care and/or poor nutrition. They can be common in stables like racing stables, where close quarters and shared equipment make the spread of lice easy.

Rain rot is an overgrowth of dermatophilosis organisms, triggered when moisture falls on dirty coats. This produces scabby crusts that follow the runoff pattern of rain on the body. Horses with light-colored coats and larger amounts of white are most susceptible. Treat with penicillin; loosen the scabs with ichthammol salve or equal parts two percent iodine and mineral oil. Shelter the horses during heavy dew months of the year.

Ringworm is a contagious fungal infection, not a parasite. They are tiny organisms that feed on plant or animal material and prefer moist, dark places like feet. This is the same as athlete's foot, and jock itch in humans. Infected areas will have hairless patches with crusts and scabs in a circular fashion. Bathe the horse using a dandruff shampoo, and be sure to wear rubber gloves. Rub off scabs and crusts, and the symptoms should start to alleviate in about a week. Disinfect tack equipment and any other communal areas.

Scratches are chapping and then cracking and crusting in the wrinkle pattern on the back of the pastern, caused by excessive drying and skin oil loss. With mild soap and water, wash thoroughly and then clip hair off the infected area, and apply zinc oxide and a bandage. Continue until new skin has grown in, and re-bandage every 2-3 days.

Sweet Itch is thickened patches with damaged hair. The areas become weepy, and the horse will scratch for relief. Sweet itch is, as the name suggests, extremely itchy. This is an allergy to flying insects. Corticosteroids may relieve itching; apply repellent at peak times.

Melanoma is a malignant (uncontrolled growth; cancerous, invasive) tumor of melanocytes (a cell that produces dark pigment). Melanomas are not uncommon in horses. However, they are mostly confined to gray, white, or other light-colored horses. During the summer months, when flying insects are most common, all horses should have a fly mask, especially light-colored horses that have pink skin around the eye.

Flying insects can lay eggs in the corners of the eye and cause numerous problems. Additionally, as in humans, horses can experience sunburns, and they may blister and peel anywhere they have pink skin. Precautions should be taken for them to have access to ample shade. Sometimes it may be necessary to confine the horses to a barn during the afternoon heat. The barn should be well-ventilated, and a cooling system may be necessary for people living in Western states.

Chapter Eight

The Equine Foot and Shoeing

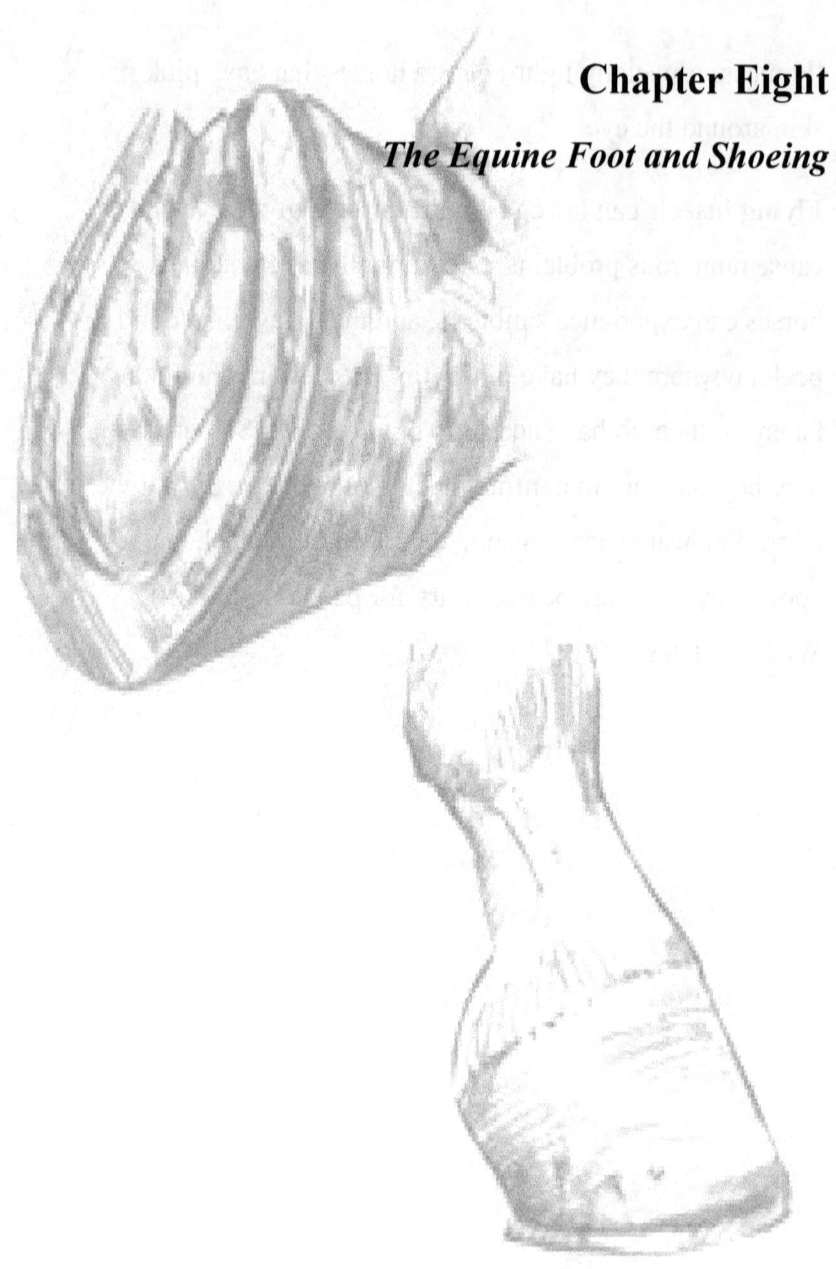

History of the Blacksmith

The Celtics formed the original custom of the lucky horseshoe. The tradition states that St. Dunstan (who eventually became Archbishop of Canterbury in 959 A.D.) was a blacksmith by trade. He once nailed a horseshoe to the Devil's hoof when asked to re-shoe the Devil's horse. This caused great pain, and after some discussion, Dustan agreed to pull the shoe as long as the Devil never set foot in a house with a horseshoe over the door. This became a lucky charm.

In the 4th century BC, the Greeks originally introduced the horseshoe. However, it does not appear to be commonly used until the middle ages. Some of the earliest shoes were made of rawhide tied on the foot. These gradually developed into modern horseshoes which are now made in a wide variety of materials, such as steel, aluminum, and plastic. Specialized shoes are made of magnesium, titanium, or copper.

The Equine Hoof

The Hoof Capsule: The Equine hoof capsule is considered a cast made of living tissue (corium) surrounding the coffin bone and lateral cartilage. As members of the mammalian family evolved from an extreme result of digitigrade progression, the Equine evolved into having a single-digit appendage encased in a tough, keratinized hoof at the end of a relativity lightweight limb. This unique feature of the Equine contributed to its speed and versatility, yet, this evolution came with a price. Limited immobility can result in crippling the horse if the connection between the hoof and bone fails.

The next section explains the individual workings of the Equine foot.

The Hoof Mechanism

The following section describes the hoof mechanism. As the horse applies weight to the foot, the frog is compressed

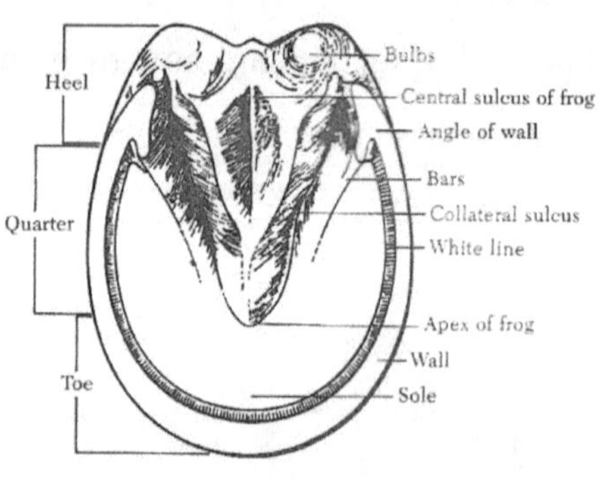

vertically and expands laterally into the sole and bars. This forces the coffin bone to descend in the hoof capsule, slightly compressing the solar corium around the solar border of the coffin bone. Around the solar corium, the central solar surface is compressed, to a smaller degree, than the corium at the solar border. Finally, the solar horn descends around the sole frog junction and the bar sole junction. The downward expansion forces the sole and bars to expand outward into the wall. It ends in the increased expansion of the wall outward.

The hoof wall expansion promotes bone-building density and releases stimulation of the coffin bone, therefore, minimizing the possibility of bone destroying shear. Shear, in this situation, would be the movement of the hoof wall parallel to the parietal (hollow part) surface of the coffin bone. Movement of this type could destroy the bone.

Compression and release are a shift in the hoof wall away from the parietal surface of the coffin bone, bearing weight during locomotion. The pressure is forced back toward the coffin bone by lifting the foot. Expansion of the wall stretches the laminar corium, enabling blood circulation and dissipating shock. As compression and expansion take place in the Equine Hoof, the frog must come in contact with the ground. This only happens if the frog is dry and free from infection (thrush). A healthy frog is full, and thick, and the central sulcus (shallow groove) must be clear and unobstructed.

The Hoof Wall

The word keratin comes from the Greek word keratos, meaning horn, which explains the horse's hoof. Keratin is the main structure of the Equine foot, which is made of soft keratins of skin, hard keratins of horn, and hair. The tubular hoof of the wall is composed of hard keratin, rich in disulphide that bonds the sole with enormous strength. The frog and white areas are rich in sulphydryl groups, which allow for superior elasticity but reduce strength.

The hoof wall grows throughout the horse's life. Constant regeneration is produced by the coronary band, where germinal cells generate populations of daughter cells, which mature and keratinize, continually adding to the proximal (origin of attachment) hoof wall.

From the coronary band to the ground surface, the keratin cells mature over eight months. These maturing keratinocytes arise from basal cells lining the holes and become organized into thin, elongated cylinders or tubules. Each hair-like tubule is continuous from its proximal origin, the coronary band, all the way to the ground surface. However, there is new evidence to prove the hoof wall does not simply grow straight down from the coronet. Most of it originates from the coronet, especially the hard-outer wall, but at least one-third of the wall is created by laminae-derived tubules called secondary epidermal laminae. They carry little cells with them as they descend the hoof, and these cells can go wherever the stress causes a weakness in the hoof.

The inter-tubular horn forms at a right angle to the tubular horn and bestows on the hoof wall the unique property of a mechanically stable, multidirectional fiber-reinforced composite.

The tubules of the Equine hoof are not arranged randomly but rather in four separate zones based on the density of tubules in the inter-tubular horn. The region of highest tubule density is the outmost layer and steadily declines towards the internal lamellar layer. In other words, the force of impact with the ground is transmitted proximally up the wall. The tubule density rises across the wall and appears to be a mechanism for smooth energy transfer from the rigid outer wall to the more plastic inner wall and ultimately to the distal phalanx.

The hoof wall has a powerful dampening function on the vibrations produced as the hoof wall makes contact with the ground during locomotion. It can reduce both the frequency and the utmost amplitude of the vibrations. By the time the shock of impact from the ground reaches the first phalanx, around ninety percent of the energy had been dissipated, mainly at the lamellar interface.

The Bars

In the past, the bars of the hoof were previously assumed to be structurally identical to the hoof wall, and just an extension of the wall turned around the frog. New studies have also proven this is not the case. Bar laminae are different from laminae elsewhere. It seems to be able to form a tubular horn and contribute to both the wall and the sole. At microscopic levels, tubules formed from the bars grew forward and migrated towards the toe. This made a significant amount of the sole come directly from the bar laminae. Note: The bar and sole corium laminae also contribute keratin cells to the sole.

The Corium

The corium or dermis was known for many years as the "quick." It is a dense matrix of tough connective tissue containing a network of arteries, veins, capillaries, and sensory and vasomotor nerves.

The corium provides the hoof with nourishment. Its dense matrix of connective tissue attaches the basement membrane of the dermal-epidermal junction to the periosteal (sheath of connective tissue surrounding bone) surface of the distal phalanx and thus suspends the distal phalanx from the inner wall of the hoof capsule.

The coronary corium saturates the coronary groove and blends distally with the lamellar corium. The inner surface is attached to the extensor tendon and cartilage of the distal phalanx by the subcutaneous (beneath the skin) tissue of the coronary cushion.

Stratum Lamellatum

The innermost layer of the hoof wall and bars is the stratum lamellatum, which can be seen at the distal short edge of the sole, becoming part of the white line.

The primary function of the innermost layer of the foot is to suspend the coffin bone within the hoof capsule; it preserves the proliferative potential for the healing of injuries. Suspension of the coffin bone and compliance of the inter digiting lamellar design helps aid in the reduction of stress and ensure even energy transfer during peak loading of the Equine foot.

The Sole

The hoof sole must be concave, enabling it to descend and expand outward into the wall. However, the important concern is the form the concavity produces. In general, from the center to the edge of the hoof, the shape is convex. Underlying hoof structures from the lateral cartilages to the coffin bone mimic such a shape. This hoof mechanism ensures the expansion is pushed outward into the wall instead of the sole being pulled outward from the wall, which could create white line separation.

Physical Functions of the Hoof

New scientific studies have shown incredible developments as to how the physical functions of the Equine hoof operate. One of the first complications horsemen face when dealing with domesticated horses is housing conditions. Certain housing environments promote unnatural surroundings, leading to severe hoof problems for the horse. Several theories have been formed to explain physiological functions. One of the most important factors is how a horse's hoof deals with vibrations from concussion. The process states: "Liquids are the best way to dissipate energy."

Hemodynamic flow is the process in which blood in the horse's feet fulfills purposes other than just providing nutrients to hoof tissues. The flow dissipates energy within the feet created during the horse's gait, such as galloping, trotting, or walking. This is a new idea of how the Equine feet respond to ground impact.

Anatomical Theories

Currently, Equine foot physiology researchers subscribe to one of two anatomical theories: pressure and depression.

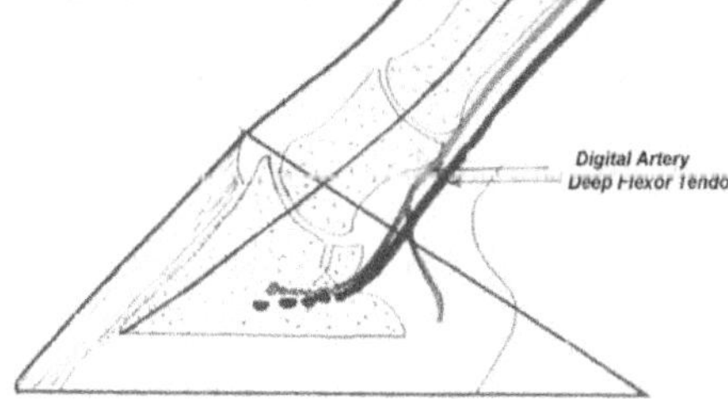

Pressure is the impact when the hoof makes contact with the ground. The concussion of impact hits the frog, stimulating the back section of the hoof to move outward.

Depression is an impact upon the ground, which forces the pastern to descend and depresses the digital cushion inside the hoof.

In both theories, hoof action pushes hoof cartilage to the outside while the digital cushion absorbs the energy. The blood is pumped from the hoof on impact with the ground. Yet, each theory indicates a single problem: In the depression or pressure state, researchers cannot show how the energy of the hoof's contact with the ground is dissipated.

The digital cushion is made of soft, elastic tissue and acts as a spring. In other words, for every action, there should be a reaction of equal force. Yet, scientific studies show that when energy measurement devices are placed into digital cushions, that does not happen. At the point when the horse's hoof is off the ground, the pressure is zero. However, after ground contact is made, the measurement should be positive, but actually, a negative pressure is created. Therefore, the hemodynamic flow suggests the negative pressure is produced by the external movement of the hoof cartilage. This change creates suction from beneath the coffin bone into the rear section of the hoof capsule. Once the blood moves to the rear of the foot through micro vessels on the side of the hoof cartilage, it dissipates the energy caused by ground impact.

Cartilaginous Cushion

Observations studied in the Equine have suggested that horses with good feet have more blood vessels in the lateral cartilage of their hooves than those with a history of foot problems. Furthermore, blood vessels in sound horses are located inside the lateral cartilage of the hoof, whereas the digital cushion in horses with problem feet is more likely to be made of cartilaginous (skeleton composition) material instead of elastic tissue.

 Environmental factors also contribute to the formation of cartilaginous digital cushions consistently, regardless of the breed in domestic horses. Areas with harder ground surfaces and higher altitudes may contribute to their formation. In regions of the country where ground surfaces are softer, more horses have digital cushions made of elastic tissue.

Currently, researchers are taking a new look at horseshoes and how they affect the shape, structure, and operation of the hoof. Metal shoes restrict the elastic flexibility of the hoof and change the trajectory of the hoof motion, adding stress to the tendons, joints, and bones in the leg. For example, scientists found in computer simulations that a peripheral load in shoed horses encouraged stresses on the coffin bone, actually warranting bone to be removed. In locomotion, the shoed horse showed the heart to stop for a split second with every beat at the fetlock. A solar load only encouraged bone to lie down or move but not be removed.

Peripheral Loading

Xenophon (350 B.C.) states, "The same care in which is given horse's feed and exercise should be given to his feet condition. Even naturally sound hoofs can be spoiled in stalls with moist, smooth floors. The floors should be sloped to avoid moisture. To prevent smoothness, stones should be sunk close to one another, each size about the same size as the hoof. The mere standing on such floors strengthens the feet."

Peripheral loading occurs when the edge of the hoof (hoof wall) bears more of the weight load. When the Equine is shoed, peripheral loading always arises since the horse focuses the weight upon the hoof wall. A shoe can, therefore, be called a peripheral loading mechanism.

Peripheral loading can be initiated in trimming the barefoot horse when the trim places additional weight on the wall. Another complication is over-trimming the hoof structures, such as the frog, sole, and bars, making it impossible to share in the weight-bearing load. Whenever the frog is not in contact with the ground, peripheral loading takes place.

Depending on the hoof's ground surface, peripheral loading varies dramatically: a hard surface increases peripheral loading, while a softer surface decreases it. For the hoof, peripheral loading is a negative situation because it severely impedes blood flow inside the hoof. Scientists discovered that harder surfaces make the blood flow faster, depleting the perfusion of tissues. Softer surfaces such as gravel, sand, or rubber pads slowed the blood flow to a trickle through small vessels, increasing tissue perfusion.

The Responsiveness of the Hoof

The Equine foot changes throughout its life. For example, the horse does not have four identical feet; each one is different from all the others due to the environment, exercise, trimming, and active stimulation of the foot. The wild horse has been a useful tool in obtaining scientific information about the hoof mechanism.

One of the greatest assets of the horse is its incredible adaptive capabilities. However, if the horse is forced to exceed these capabilities, lameness occurs. Studies have shown the Equine has found a method of dealing with the stresses of domestication by increasing the number of laminae in the hoof where problems arise. This sign has given horsemen the ability to establish evidence of when a horse is overstressed.

In the foot, fewer laminae are better, and indications of extra laminae show stress has arisen in the horse. The problem with extra laminae is they become longer and thinner, increasing the chance of laminitis. There is no information on whether or not shod horses have more laminae than barefoot horses, yet the symptoms are prevalent and the risks are increased dramatically by shoeing. However, shod horses with toe clips do have more laminae around these clips, meaning we can mechanically increase the density of laminae.

In normal circumstances, there are more laminae on the flared side of the hoof as well as the toes. There are also more laminae in front of a sole callous; the pillar edge of a sole callous appears to be a stress area. This proves that laminae are created in response to stress, but it appears that the hoof horn is affected as well. In the foot, hoof tubules change direction according to load and stress in the hoof wall.

Equines have the ability to react not only to their environment, but the hoof is so responsive that changes can also be seen in the physical contact area of the hoof between standing on concrete and standing on rubber. The hoof wall is hard and fluid but moves. For example, when the horse is standing on rubber, there is a little more exterior surface area of the foot, which drastically reduces the pressure inside the hoof capsule. There is only one-third of the amount of pressure on the hoof wall when standing on rubber versus standing on concrete.

Necessity of Movement

Time and time again, veterinarians come back to the health of the foot. This concept has been a consistent theme of natural hoof care activists, but finally, there is scientific evidence to prove the claims.

Profusion is a measurable quantity of something. Movement improves the blood perfusion of the foot. Consistent motion is the only way the horse can develop the fibro-cartilage in the back of the hoof. For example, leaving a young horse housed with minimal exercise and movement will likely cause poor hoof conditions to develop and carry on through its lifetime.

Field studies using pedometer devices measured the movement patterns of horse groups living in two to three-acre housing environments and discovered that the healthiest horses walked an average of four to six thousand steps a day, approximately three to five miles. On the other hand, horses in stalled environments only walked eight hundred steps per day.

Hoof Growth

Exposure to constant wet environments allows the horse's feet to grow without wear, leading to misalignments in the natural balance of the hoof. Proper trimming and shoeing will maintain the correct balance for each horse.

If excess amounts of grain and alfalfa are fed, the additional amount of protein is absorbed by the body and can lead to imbalances that promote poor hoof conditions, along with active subclinical (beneath, not determined) laminitis. The horse's owner should ensure they have adequate information when choosing their proper diet.

Confirmation

Confirmation faults are the most common reason for shoeing a horse. These confirmation problems originate from abnormal stresses that were explained above, along with genetic defaults.

Genetic faults so severe they change the natural way in which the horse travels must be corrected by proper trimming and shoeing. However, bone structure defects cannot be corrected by shoeing.

The professional farrier must understand all varieties of the horse's gait, as well as how to influence movement to keep the interference of physiological function and damage to the hoof wall minimal.

Balance of the hoof is determined by the horizontal level when the horse is in motion. This is done through centering the horse in the middle of the hoof and placing the coronary band level with the ground.

The hoof angle is determined by degrees that directly correlate with the angle of the shoulder. The horse's hind feet have a two to three-degree greater angle. Misalignment of angles in the horse's leg can cause irreversible damage to the bones, muscles, and tendons.

Choosing a Ferrier

Professional farriers (blacksmiths, a specialist in Equine hoof care) have always viewed horseshoes as an aid to protect the horse's hooves from a variety of conditions brought on by domestication. Nevertheless, when the horseshoe was first designed, the scientific study of anatomy and physiology had not been invented yet. So, the ill effects on the Equine foot could never be completely understood.

Obtaining a qualified farrier requires some obligations by the owner. The first step is a systematic approach. This will result in a rewarding relationship for both horse owners and farrier. However, there are some guidelines the horse owner needs to be aware of:

- Is the farrier professional and courteous?
- Does the farrier arrive on time and on the scheduled day?
- Do they treat the horse with respect?
- Is the farrier willing to answer all the owner's questions with knowledge and skill?
- Will they keep an appointment book?
- Will the farrier discuss discipline approaches with the horse?

When the farrier arrives to shoe or trim the horses, there are several pieces of equipment necessary to perform this activity.

Farrier's Tools

- ➢ Anvil
- ➢ Nail or alligator clincher
- ➢ Hoof stand and hoof rest for older or injured horses
- ➢ Ferrier's knife, sole knife
- ➢ Apron
- ➢ Hoof pick
- ➢ Clinch cutter
- ➢ Driving hammer
- ➢ Rounding hammer
- ➢ Nipper
- ➢ Hoof parer, pincers
- ➢ Divider
- ➢ Clinch block
- ➢ Shoeing box
- ➢ Shoe spreader
- ➢ Hoof leveler
- ➢ Rasp
- ➢ Adequate supply of shoes and nails

Shoeing Process

To properly shoe or trim a horse, the following guidelines should be followed. The process starts with foot preparation, preparing the shoe, fitting the shoe, nailing the shoe, and finishing the hoof.

Hoof preparation is step one of the farrier's job. This is done by leveling the horse's foot so it makes full contact with a flat shoe or the ground.

Balance is subjective to several criteria, which are: the horse stands in the middle of the hoof, the coronary band is level with the ground, and the hoof lands flat while the horse is in motion. However, this may not be possible to visualize in all activities.

Angle is the next step; the hoof angle is parallel to the horse's shoulder. Hoof angles are subject to the internal structures of the foot, such as the coffin bone and lateral cartilage. Hoof deviations from pastern to shoulder angles are due to improper nipping or rasping.

Hoof length will vary with each breed of horse and depend on the horse's activities.

Preparing the sole is done neatly and smoothly; excessive paring and rasping can weaken the bars and sole. Correction to the frog and bulbs should also be cut neat and smooth, although only when necessary.

Dressing the hoof wall itself is done to flatten and smooth the wall, coronary band, flares, and return the foot to a natural shape.

Finally, evaluating the balance, angles, and levels is done to ensure corrections are made properly. Not all corrections can be made at one time; therefore, it may be necessary to achieve this goal over several consistent sessions.

Shoe quality is the next process, which means the shoe is flat in all aspects. From the center of the toe to the center of the heel, the shoe must be in a perpendicular line unless corrective shoeing is being applied.

Heel cut angles are parallel to the hoof angle.

Fullering (semicircular cross-section, used for grooving metal) is the last step. Fullering starts slightly before the toe nail and ends just past the heel nail. The position of the fullering allows the nails to exit on the white line. Nail holes are spaced evenly from toe to quarters unless hoof conditions prevent proper spacing. They are never placed over the white line.

The shape of the shoe is determined by the white line of the foot. There are varying degrees of error in fitting the shoe, such as the toe being too narrow or wide, causing the hoof not to follow the bend to the quarters.

If the heels are not trimmed properly, they will can compromise movement. Full contact with the hoof wall should be made with the shoe unless pieces of the hoof wall are missing.

Sole pressure is determined by the width of the shoe. No more than one-eighth inch of the hoof surface of the shoe should make contact with the sole.

The seat of the corns is pared so as not to make contact with the shoe. If the horse is flat-soled, the shoe should be concave. Excessive paring on the sole can cause temporary lameness.

Expansion is the part of the shoe that is seen on the outside of the horse's hoof. Proper expansion is a dime's width from toe to heel and two dimes' width on the heel of the shoe. Adjusting the heel length is extending beyond the buttress and the bars, and there should be the same distance left for the expansion of the heel.

Once the shoe is fitted, the next step is nailing the shoe to the horse's hoof. Nails exit the hoof wall one-third inch from the bottom of the foot and precede level ascending toward the toe. All clinches are square and set into the wall, in line with the nail shaft. Improper clinching will not hold the shoe in place for a serviceable period.

Finally, the finished hoof should be rasped just above the clinch line to ensure all sharp edges are smoothed, avoiding injury to the horse.

Caution: If the horseman has chosen the barefoot course for their horse, the horse should be trimmed with a Mustang-type roll.

A Mustang roll encourages the expansion of the wall and reduces the portion of weight borne by the wall, shifting weight more to the sole and frog. The hoof wall and laminar corium alone are not strong enough to bear the horse's weight. Poor trims can cause the coronet band to be forced upward, therefore exposing the horse to harder terrain and requiring a more aggressive roll to keep the balance between the wall and sole.

Reference: Robert M. Bowker VMD, Ph.D.,
Professor of Anatomy, Michigan State University College of Veterinary Medicin

Chapter Nine

Horse Tack and Equipment

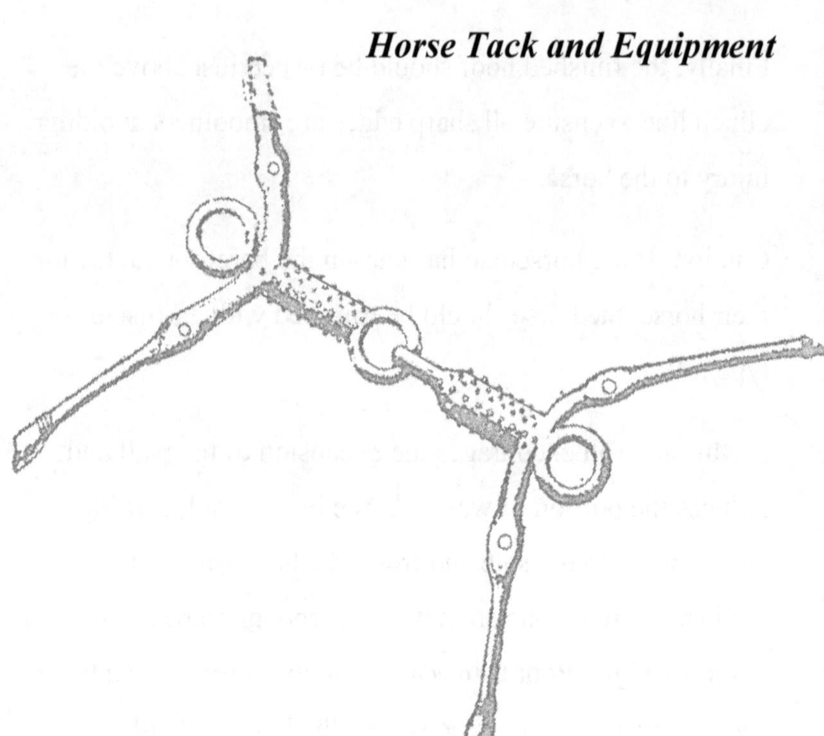

History of Horse Transportation

The first form of road transportation started with humans carrying goods on their heads in pots, oxen as pack animals, and finally, horses. Vehicles did not come into use until about 5000 B.C.; the first was called a travois (a frame used to drag loads). These were most likely pulled by bullocks (castrated cattle).

Later in ancient Mesopotamia, the wheel appeared on a two-wheeled cart. Four-wheeled wagons appeared in about 2500 B.C. Horse harnesses were developed about 2000 B.C. and used for two-wheeled chariots. Collars and breeching did not come about until 1650 B.C. in Egypt. Of course, this invention enabled horses to pull faster and carry more weight. For example, in modern terms, a heavy draft horse weighing 2000lb can pull about 1.5 tons and up to 9 tons depending on conditions; however, with a wheeled vehicle on the pavement, they can pull three to eight times their weight.

Horses and Warfare

There is controversy over whether or not horses were ridden or driven first. Ancient bridles have been discovered dating back to 3500-3000 B.C., nearly as soon as the domestication of the horse. Archeological sites show evidence of bit wear on the teeth of fossils. In these same sites, various types of bridles and bits used were found. Some of the first bits were made of rope, bone, or hard wood. Metal bits came into use in the 2nd century BC, originally designed for bronze.

Once the Equine became an instrument for man's survival, human warfare would be forever changed. By using a fundamental principle for choosing a warhorse the conformation of "form to function" are essential. Therefore, the type of horse used for warfare would be chosen for the task at hand. Was the knight facing battle, individual combat, or reconnaissance? However, there was a trade-off for speed or protection. Adding weight minimizes speed but increases protection. Therefore, the favorite war horse of the knights during the Middle Ages was the Destrier because they had the size for added protection as well as the speed and endurance needed for combat.

To improve a knights' fighting skills, they participated in a martial competition known as jousting. Jousting became extremely popular due to the large sums of money to be made by winning. However, many knights lost their lives during these battles: for example, Henry II of France died when a shard from his opponent's broken lance went through the visor into his eye. The maneuver was termed "tilting." This tactic encompassed charging at a high rate of speed, intending to unhorse the opponent by killing or disabling him. The first recorded jousting tournament appeared in about 1066 AD.

Equine Tack

History of the Saddle

Many knights competed with only a pad resembling an English saddle. Saddles were not widely used until the 2nd

century. These original saddles were designed for warfare, which made the horse an irreplaceable creature in the evolution of human beings. The saddle allowed for additional weight by distributing the mass in a less obtrusive manner. Saddles made many advances in the coming years, but none as instrumental as the McClellan saddles, introduced in the 1830s. They were originally designed for the Calvary and used for over 150 years. The style remained constant until 1859. However, the invention of the stirrup did not occur until 322 A.D. in the Jin Dynasty of China. The stirrup enabled the soldier to have a wide range of movement while mounted on the horse's back. Few inventions as simple as the stirrup has created such an influence on society.

Components of the Saddle

Today there are two major types of saddles: English and Stock. The most critical component defining the saddle is the tree, which can be made of many different materials, like rawhide, wood, and modern synthetic products. The saddle tree defines the shape, length, and width of the finished product. Saddle trees are designed to distribute the weight of the rider evenly, eliminating pressure points that may cause damage to the horse's back.

Western saddles have leather stretched over the pommel of the tree. This will eventually support the horn and cantle. The seat is then made to form to the horse's back, giving the rider a place to sit. Attached to the tree are the stirrup leathers and saddle skirts. Sheepskin is used to line the underside of the saddle and protect the horse from sores.

The English saddle is used for English riding events, such as show jumping, hunt seat, dressage, saddle seat, horse racing, and polo. The most significant difference in an English saddle is, of course, the lack of a saddle horn. They are flatter in appearance and have a self-padding design of panels. The length of flaps, depth of seat, and height of the cantle play a particular role in the event in which the saddle is intended to be used. The tree of an English saddle is called a "spring tree" because they are semi-adjustable. Although they have minimal flexibility.

Physical Characteristics of the Horse

History shows it's impossible to have a perfect fit between the horse and saddle. Think of the working cowboy; he could not afford to buy a new saddle every time he changed his horse. Yet, if his saddle caused the boss's horse saddle sores, he did not have a job long. Therefore, a high-quality

saddle was a necessity for the working cowboy. As a horse advances in training, age, and condition, so do the back muscles and even the underlying skeletal system. This makes it necessary to make periodic adjustments. Some key physical characteristics affect a saddle fit. The following list explains the characteristics.

Shape of withers: Ideally, the withers should be level with, or slightly above, the highest point of the rump (croup).

Shape of the back: A horse with a narrow back or flat back can find a saddle to be uncomfortable. A young horse that runs downhill can end up with the saddle slipping forward.

Length of the back: Horses with a shorter than average back can find the saddle skirts digging into their backs, loins, and kidneys.

Prominence of the shoulders: Large-shouldered horses can be constricted by an ill-fitting saddle, as it forces the shoulders against the tree bars. Thin-shouldered horses may find the saddle riding forward onto the shoulder blades.

With the horse standing on level ground, place the saddle on the horse's back. Saddles are designed to fit the horse's anatomy. In a lot of circumstances, it is not a poorly fitting saddle but rather an improper positioning. When the saddle is sitting in the correct place, the cinch will fall four inches behind the elbow.

Check the distance at the withers. There should be a clearance of two to four fingers stacked between the withers and gullet without a saddle pad.

Next is the shoulder clearance at the withers. There should be room to slide your fingers between the saddle sheepskin and the shoulder. Ideally, this should also be done when a rider is mounted in the saddle.

The saddle skirting will follow the contour of the horse's back. It should not extend past its loins.

Finally, check the balance. View the horse from the side; the flat area of the seat should be level. Along with the fork, it should not be higher than the cantle. Once the saddle is cinched, the saddle should never lift off the horse's back.

The ultimate goal is to not only fit the horse but also add to the rider's comfort. A properly fit saddle will make a tremendous difference in the rider's equitation abilities. Being adjusted in the horse's center of balance allows the rider to stay in their center of gravity.

Fitting the Rider to the Saddle

The seat of a saddle is one way to determine its size. Seat sizes are measured in half-inch increments and range from 12" to 17". However, this has little to do with fit. The depth and angle of the seat, the slope and dish of the cantle, and the style and angle of the fork, all combined with the seat size, determine how much room is available in a particular seat. As a rule of thumb, so to speak, allow four inches between the rider and the fork (pommel) of the saddle. The rider's seat should not rest on top of the cantle or against the back of the cantle. In general, it is better to have the saddle be a smidge too large than too small.

The Bit

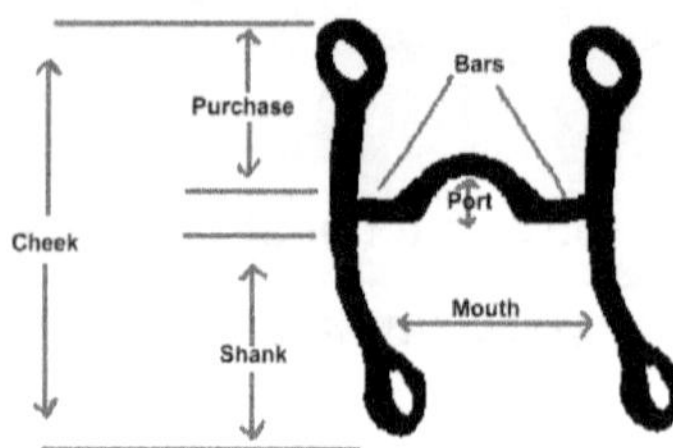

Bits consist of two basic components: the purchase and the rings of a snaffle or the shanks of a curb. All bits act with some combination of pressure and leverage, often in conjunction with a curb chain, cavesson, or pressure applied to the poll (located at the second vertebrae, between the horse's ears) from a headstall. To place the horse in the correct bit, as well as fit the rider with a bit that matches their experience, it is essential to understand the Equine mouth.

Types of Bits

- ➢ Basic bit types include:
- ➢ Snaffle bit
- ➢ Curb bit
- ➢ Pelham bit
- ➢ Kimberwicke
- ➢ Gag bit
- ➢ Double bridle (carries two bits) or Weymouth
- ➢ Hackamores or Bosals (do not use a mouthpiece)
- ➢ Modern bits consist of several types of materials, for example:
- ➢ Stainless Steel is the most common material.
- ➢ Copper warms quickly in the horse's mouth but does not last as long as stainless steel.
- ➢ Copper Alloy is a combination of copper and stainless steel. This style promotes salivation and extends the life of the bit.
- ➢ Sweet Iron easily rusts and provides an improved taste, as well as better salivation.
- ➢ Brass Alloy has the same results as copper alloy and is less expensive to produce.

Aluminum is considered to be a bad choice for mouthpieces. This type of mouthpiece should be avoided, so note that cheap bits are made with aluminum.

Bit Mouthpiece

Bits are designed to work with pressure, not pain. The type of bit determines where the pressure can be brought to bear: the bars, tongue, and or roof of the mouth, as well as the lips, chin groove, and poll. Bits offer varying degrees of control and communication between rider and horse, depending upon their design and the skill of the rider. Horses' bits are designed in two categories, the first being snaffles and the second being curbs. A particular mouthpiece does not make the type of bit. It is the leverage applied by the cheekpieces or shanks that determine if a bit is in the family of snaffle or curb.

Bits are designed with several types of mouthpieces, such as:

- ➢ Single jointed
- ➢ Double jointed
- ➢ Mullen (straight bar)
- ➢ Arched port in the center of varying height

All of these types of mouthpieces will be made with one of three textures: smooth, roughened, or twisted. The following is a list of mouthpiece designs.

The Gag mouthpiece uses cheek leverage (a curb chain is not used) to increase the severity. Therefore, there is no true leverage. The bit works with pressure applied to the lips and poll simultaneously.

Pressure applied to the lips tends to make the horse raise their head. This can be useful for the horse that has been taught or learned to get behind the bit. This means that the horse evades pressure by running off. Some believers feel that the increased poll pressure will encourage the horse to drop its head, but this is not the case. Horses naturally move away from pressure, and since the lips are extremely sensitive, the horse will initially raise its head until it learns to give to pressure. Gag bits are popular and used in speed events, mainly for increased control. There are several different designs of the gag bit.

Gag Snaffles are similar in shape to a snaffle, except for mouthpiece rings on either side. Each bit ring has two holes: one ring on top of the bottom ring. Gag cheekpieces have a round piece of leather or rope that runs through these holes. At the end of the cheekpiece, after they pass through both holes, is one metal ring, to which the rein attaches. When rein pressure is applied, the bit slides upward and rotates slightly in the mouth. Severity is determined by the size of the rings; the larger the ring, the more severe the gag. There are two main styles of snaffle gags: The Balding gag, which has a loose-ring design, and the   Cheltenham gag, which has an eggbutt design.

Important: The "gag snaffle" is not a snaffle bit, although they offer an option of acting like one if the rider only attaches a rein to the bit rings and not to the sliding gag cheekpieces. Gags are fitted similarly to the snaffle; therefore, they should be used with two reins when possible, using the gag only when needed.

The Elevator Gag is designed with a snaffle mouthpiece, and cheeks or shanks are attached to the side. The upper shank has a hole to attach the cheekpiece of the bridle, and the lower shank has several holes to attach the rein. The lower rings of the shanks apply more leverage, increasing the severity of the bit. When rein pressure is applied, rotation of the mouthpiece places pressure on the poll as the upper shank moves forward, putting pressure on the lips.

Dutch/Continental/Three–ring/Four-ring/Pessoa is Gag is similar to the elevator, except for the cheekpieces that consist of stacked rings. There is usually one ring above the mouthpiece, to which the cheekpiece is attached. The ring below is attached directly to the mouthpiece and acts similar to the snaffle. The lower ring or rings, of which there are usually two, are where the reins are attached. The second ring applies the gag action. The lower second ring is placed on the stack for more leverage. Dutch gags are useful because they provide options for the severity of the bit. The bridle cheek pieces are attached to the top rings to produce pressure.

American Gag is an "H" shaped bit with one ring on the upper shank to attach the bridle. The lower is the gag ring, as well as a middle ring attaching the snaffle rein. The American gag can slide up the curves of the bit shanks as pressure is applied by the reins. Pressure is put on the corners of the mouth, encouraging the horse to raise its head. The American gag does not offer optional rein adjustments.

Half-ring/Duncan Gag, this type of gag, is particularly severe. The ring ends have holes through which the cheekpieces run. Unlike the snaffle gag, no holes for a snaffle rein exist. Therefore, only the gag rein can be used.

Ported Mouthpieces

Ported Mouthpieces include several types of bits, along with many driving bits. In the middle of the mouthpiece, there is a "port" or curve, which will vary in height. Ported bit actions are directly related to the height of the port. Low ports provide some tongue relief, while larger ports press hard on the palate (roof of the mouth) when the reins are pulled. Once rein pressure is applied, the port acts as a fulcrum and transfers the pressure onto the bars. Recent research has shown that the port must be two to two and a half inches or more in height for it to touch the palate. Ported bits are popular in Western disciplines. The most common mouthpiece is the Kimberwicke and Pelhams.

Jointed Mouthpieces

Jointed mouthpieces are the most common in snaffles but are seen in all bit families. Jointed mouthpieces can have one or more of the following: a joint or joints in the center, with or without a roller. The joint breaks upward toward the top of the mouth, applying direct pressure. When used with leverage pressure from a shank or cheekpiece, the pressure is forced outward toward the front of the mouth.

Single-jointed mouthpieces apply pressure to the tongue, lips and minimal pressure to the bars. Due to the V-shape of the bit, when pressure is applied, the mouthpiece contracts and causes a nutcracker effect, thus pinching the bars, which pushes into the sensitive roof of the mouth if used harshly.

Caution must be taken not to mistake the Tom Thumb snaffle, or cowboy snaffle, as these bits are curb bits and operate with leverage. When rein pressure is applied, the horse is subjected to both the nutcracker effect and leverage of the curb, which also causes the joint to rotate and apply pressure to the tongue. Therefore, such bits can be very harsh, particularly in the hands of an inexperienced rider. This type of mouthpiece is one of the most common, used in all equestrian activities.

Double-jointed bits conform better to the horse's "U" shaped mouth because they minimize or eliminate the nutcracker effect. Some double-jointed mouthpieces are designed with rollers, helping the young green horses learn to relax during the Bitting process.

The French Link includes the snaffle, gag, Pelham, curb, and driving bits. The mouthpiece has two joints and a central link. This link is flat, short, and bone-shaped, with rounded corners. The French link is one of the milder mouthpieces; the two joints reduce the nutcracker effect and encourage relaxation. However, the French link tends to pinch the tongue, causing pain to the horse. The bit pressure is applied to the lips, tongue, and bars of the mouth. The mouthpiece is commonly seen in snaffles rather than gags, pelhams, or curbs. French links are used regularly in dressage work, as well as many English-style disciplines. It is rarely seen in Western-style activities.

Roller Joints are similar to the French link, except for the roller. On either side of the roller is a joint, which eliminates any nutcracker effect. This eliminates the nutcracker effect and allows the horse to relax without the stress of pinching the bars and pushing harshly on the roof of the mouth. This style of bit is common in any discipline and is also permitted in dressage.

Ported Link is also similar to a French link, except the middle link has a slight upward curve, like a port. The upward curve allows more room for the tongue, which also encourages salivation and reduces stress levels on any horse. It is common in many snaffles but used in all styles of bits designed, as well as riding disciplines.

Broken Segunda is a snaffle, usually with a Dee-ring. This is similar to the ported link, except the middle link is much higher and makes a clear upside-down "U." The Segunda is supposed to encourage the horse to soften and stay light on the bridle, but the "U" shape can be quite sharp, and even dig into the tongue to the point of cutting it. This is another example where training cannot be replaced by a more severe bit. Therefore, they are best suited for a skilled rider with light contact.

Multi–jointed are bits with more than two joints. They tend to wrap around the lower jaw of the horse. In general, multi-joints allow for more pressure points, with lighter contact on the horse's mouth. Some consider this to be a more severe bit; however, lighter contact means less pressure has to be used to achieve the desired response.

The Waterford mouthpiece is made with five to nine joints and is very flexible. The general idea behind the design is that great flexibility will discourage the horse from leaning on the bit. English disciplines prefer the type of bit, allowing greater control for strong horses being used to jump or event. The bit mouthpiece is rare in a Pelham and curb.

Caution the bits explained in the following section are not recommended for use under any circumstance. Training can never be replaced by the use of a more severe bit. However, I feel an informed reader can make an accurate assessment.

- ➢ The Chain Saw/Chain
- ➢ Twisted/Serrated Wire
- ➢ Double-Single Twisted Wire
- ➢ Double Mouth/Scissors/ W or Y Mouth

Bit Shanks

The Cyclopedia in 1728 referred to shanks or cheeks as branches, as outlined in the paragraph below:

"The branches of a bridle, in manage of horses, are two crooked pieces of iron, which support the mouth bit, the chain, and the curb. These are fastened on one side to the headstall, on the other to the reins. Serving to keep the horse's head under command. Whichever way the branches of the bit incline, the horse's mouth always goes the contrary. The branch is always to be accommodated to the design, either, of bringing in, or raising the horse's head, and to the degree. Accordingly, there are strong and hardy branches that are either straight, in the form of a pistol, for a young horse, to form their mouth; or, after the constable of France's fashion, for knee; others in the French fashion, etc."

The following three rules apply.

- ➢ The farther the branch is from the horse's neck, the more effect it will have.
- ➢ The short branches, ceteris paribus, are ruder, and their effects are more sudden than those of others.
- ➢ The branches are proportioned to the length of the horse's neck.

The length of the bit shank determines the amount of leverage placed on the horse's head and mouth. The term shank is generally used to describe the entire sidepiece of a bit, commonly termed "cheek."

The shank is the lever arm of the bit, extending down from the mouthpiece to the rein rings. The purchase is the upper portion of the cheek, which extends to the headstall rings. All shanks have rein rings at the bottom for the curb chain and cheek rings to attach the bridle.

The average leverage ratio for a typical curb bit is 1:3, in that one ounce of pressure by the rider results in three ounces of pressure in the horse's mouth. The relative ratio between the length of the purchase and the lever arm also affects the amount and type of leverage applied to the chin and poll of the horse.

Shanks Are Designed in Two Classifications

Loose jawed allows the shank to swivel at the point where the mouthpiece attaches to the cheek. This, therefore, allows a more subtle communication between the rider and horse.

Fixed jawed are molded into the shank itself, decreasing communication between the horse and rider.

 Cheek angles come in three options:

The straight up and down shank is typically used for horses that maintain a vertical head position, such as dressage horses and Western pleasure horses.

The curved shank is for horses that have a nose out position when working, such as cutting and roping horses. These curved shanks are sometimes called "grazing" bits; however, a horse should never be allowed to graze with a bit. The term came from the mistaken notion that the shanks were curved back to allow the horse to graze. In reality, the design simply allows the horse to travel comfortably with its nose well ahead of the vertical position.

The "S" curve in a shank has no major effect on the angle in which the rein engages but alters the balance of the bit at the point where the lever arm joins the mouthpiece.

Long and Short Shanks

Short-shanked bits are considered milder and better suited for the young horse transitioning from a snaffle to a curb. There is less pressure applied to the horse's head once they reach a proper collected position.   However, the shorter shanked bits apply pressure quicker to the horse's mouth and are not well suited for polishing the finished horse. The finished horse requires quieter communication from the rider.

Longer shank bits rotate back further before contact is made with the horse's mouth. Therefore, the horse is given ample warning of the rider's hand movements, allowing them time to respond before any significant pressure is applied to the mouth.

Long Lower Shanks and Long Upper Shanks

A long lower shank (lever arm) increases the leverage and, thus, the pressure on the chin groove and bars of the mouth. This design is better suited for the longer-necked horse, as it encourages the horse to drop its head down and bring its nose perpendicular to the ground (a collected position). Overall, the design is for the finished horse.

A long upper shank works by increasing poll pressure without applying as much pressure to the bars of the mouth. Therefore, this design is better suited for the short thick-necked horse, as it encourages the horse to drop its head and collect to the proper position.

Correctional Bits

There are many factors used in the Bitting equation which must be considered to get a true assessment of the proper bit. A common misconception is the term "correction bit" (a euphemism for severe) or training bit (implying a mild bit), as the terms are relative. The Equine bit is designed to rest on the horse's bars in their mouth; a heavy-handed rider can severely damage the bars, causing distress to the horse. Correctional bits were designed to improve a horse's performance. Once the problem is corrected, the use of the bit should be discontinued. However, only experienced riders should consider the use of correctional bits, as in some cases, misuse can cause an escalation of the initial problems.

Hackamores and Bosals

The true hackamore is derived from the Spanish word ja'quima. This is most often used to start colts. The hackamore (bosal) applies direct pressure to the nose and chin. Hackamore bridles and reins are made of rope, leather, or horsehair, and the bosal is constructed of rawhide. The bosal hackamore must be fitted properly around the nose. The bosal should not be confused with the hackamore bit; these usually have long shanks and can place extreme pressure on the horse's nose, chin groove, and poll with a small amount of pressure applied to the reins.

Bridles and Reins

The most common bridle consists of a crown piece (over the horse's head), cheekpiece (attaches to the bit), and browband (around the horse's forehead). They are made of various types of materials, such as leather, nylon, rope, or synthetics.

The reins are also made in various types and styles. The three most common types are as follows: split, rope, and romal.

Split reins, as can be deduced from the name, have one single rein attached to each side of the bit. They vary from six to eight feet in length and one-half inch to five eights inch thick. Harness leather is recommended because of its weight.

Rope reins are a particular favorite for roping, barrel racing, and other speed events. Single reins are especially popular for children because one rein cannot be dropped on the ground while riding, and they can be adjusted to length to ensure safety for the child.

Romal reins are mainly used for Western pleasure show horses. The romal rein is a single rein with a "tail" tying the reins together.

Curb Chains

Curb chains rest in the chin groove, applying pressure to the horse when communication is activated by the rein. Different curbs require proper adjustments.

Curb chains that are too loose will pinch the horse in the corners of the mouth and not allow the bit to function as designed. If the curb chain is overly tight, it will force the horse's mouth to open due to the increase in pressure. A general rule to apply after the horse is bridled is to use the two index fingers between the curb chain and chin groove of the horse; the fit should be snug but not tight. The use of chain or leather is adequate.

Horse Equipment

Halter: When purchasing a halter, first choose the color, type, and size. Halters are normally made large and can be purchased one size smaller to have an appropriate fit. Sizes range from weanling, yearling, pony, small, medium, large, extra-large, draft, and mule. The halter should be the correct size to fit the horse.

Lead Ropes: Lead ropes are also made of many types of materials. When purchasing a lead rope, it should be at least five-eighths inch in diameter and six to eight feet long. Cotton is preferred over nylon. Cotton is soft and supple and will help to eliminate rope burns to the handler. However, nylon will last longer and is harder to break.

Grooming Box: Horses do not require grooming; although, regularly groomed horses will have better and more attractive coats. However, grooming is a necessity before riding the horse to remove any dirt and material that would cause chafing or pain. This also allows the handler to check for any injuries on the horse.

Proper grooming is a multiple-step process, and you will need some tools to perform this function. Beyond the basic equipment for grooming, there are thousands of products available on the market, from hoof polish, mane and tail rubber bands, tail socks, hair polish for extra shine, etc.

Bathing the horse is also something horses do not require. Many horses live their entire life without ever having a bath. Most horses object to water at first and must be trained to accept bathing. Bathing will assist in cooling the horse after a heavy workout and remove sweat and dirt. A moist sponge can be used to wash the horse's face, and a scraper or brush can be used to remove excess water.

Curry comb: The curry comb is either rubber or metal. Rubber curries are less harsh on the horse's skin and should not be used on the legs or head. During spring, when the horses are shedding, a shedding comb can be used to remove loose hair. Curry is done in a circular motion all over the main part of the body to loosen embedded materials.

Dandy brush: This is a stiff bristled brush to be used on the legs and head. Caution must be used when brushing the head; some horses may object to having their head brushed with a stiff bristled brush.

Body brush: This is a medium bristled brush that will adequately remove all loose dirt and material on the body. Brush the hair in short strokes until the horse is clean.

Hoof pick: The hoof pick is for all four feet which need to be cleaned and checked regularly.

Fly spray: This is used primarily in the summer months. Spray the horse holding the bottle four to six inches away, and be sure to cover the legs and face. Then brush the horse with a soft brush to spread the spray evenly over its body. In some parts of the country, caution must be taken to remove botfly eggs. (Bot eggs are yellow, roughly the size of a grain of sand. They will be stuck to the hairs on the body and usually can be removed with your fingernail or a dull knife.)

Mane and tail brush or comb: These are used to properly brush or comb the horse's mane and tail. Start at the bottom and slowly work to the top of the tail or crest of the neck. Pick up small pieces of hair at a time until the whole tail or mane is completely brushed.

Clippers or scissors: It is preferred by some people to clip a small section of the horse's mane called a "bridle path," just behind the horse's ears about four to six inches long, leaving the forelock.

Chapter Ten

Natural Horsemanship

To completely understand the concepts about to be explained in the following sections, please see Chapter Two: Equine Behavior.

Environmental Effects

Since the dawn of time, eohippus evolved as a herd animal. This survival developed one of the most unique abilities of the horse: sensory perception.

Sensory - Any faculty by which a human or animal obtains information about the physical world around them.

Perception – An attitude or understanding based on what is observed or thought.

The horse is one of the most perceptive beings on earth. One simple alteration or the smallest movement in the surrounding area heightens their senses. Due to the sensory perceptions of the Equine, two foundational methods were developed by natural horsemanship equestrian professionals. The first starts with evolution, and the second is imprinting at the birth of a new foal.

Evolution began with sixty million years of growth, transforming the horse into an intelligent, agile, willing creature created by God to be man's servant. The basis for natural horsemanship is training techniques that avoid abusive behavior.

Imprinting starts at birth; for instance, when a mare nuzzles and licks the foal dry, Epimeletic Behavior bonds the two for life. Herd imprinting starts the evolutionary instincts that develop the social bonds necessary for survival.

Responses

The term response refers to a specific type of behavior. In this case, movement. To the horseman, responses are the act of the desired movement. The most important factor to remember when asking for a response from the horse is to expect small precise movements, one step at a time. That will gradually lead to the finished maneuvers. For example:

The initial reaction of a horse to bit pressure is to pull away. Steady contact is continued until the horse gives to pressure applied by the bit. In other words, the horse brings their nose down and toward the chest. Nevertheless, do not expect all the steps to be completed in one lesson.

Stimuli

Stimulus refers to something that encourages activity to begin a process. Stimuli are categorized in two ways: conditioned or unconditioned.

Conditioned: A stimulus that has to be learned through practice. This is when direct rein pressure is applied; the horse is shown which direction to respond and learns this quickly.

Unconditioned: A stimulus that naturally causes a response with no prior practice. This is when teaching a horse to neck rein, the new cue or stimulus is applied with a slight lapse, then followed by the basic cue or conditioned stimulus. Once the bearing rein is applied, the correct response will be made by the horse, ensued by the release in rein pressure.

These stimuli are commonly referred to as cues. Remember, very few cues are learned from a natural stimulus. For example, any stimulus must contain a level of specificity for the horse to decipher the correct response. The Equine can receive stimuli through several sensory systems; however, the most effective method for the horseman to communicate with a horse is using tactile and/or vocal stimuli. Voice commands and pressure have developed into the basic forms of horsemanship. However, cues must be presented indiscriminately. A rider cannot use poor, inconsistent techniques with a horse and then apply discriminate and specific cues at a later date, expecting the horse to identify the difference.

Reinforcements

Natural training uses the principle of certain reinforcements to obtain specific responses. This is done only through patience and perfection. So, over a given period, the learning abilities of the horse can be developed. These reinforcements are categorized into several categories.

Secondary Reinforcements

Secondary reinforcements are learned by the horse over a given period; for instance, the training secession will end if the horse performs well. The trainer who can condition the horse for secondary reinforcement has another tool to work with.

Negative Reinforcement

Negative reinforcement is aversive stimuli that a horse will work to avoid, given the choice. There are at least three different options when training with negative reinforcement.

Acquisition is a negative reinforcement. The horse chooses a response in the absence of a cue, resulting in discipline. The punishment must be immediate and accurate. The goal is not the acquisition of a new response but rather the weakening or elimination of a previous repertoire. This type of negative response by the horseman is traditionally used to correct bad habits or vices. The most effective punishments must cause the horse to select a desirable alternate response that leads to reward.

Escape: The adverse stimuli are applied with little or no cue and independently of the horse's response. To ask a horse for movement to the right, pressure from the left leg must be applied, forcing the horse to move away from the pressure, thus escaping from the adverse stimuli.

Avoidance: When a cue is given, and the correct response is made by the horse, no punishment is necessary. If the response is incorrect or latent, then adverse stimulus or negative reinforcement is applied. When the horse is asked to back up, only light pressure is utilized to start, and then if the horse's response is latent or refused, then heavier pressure is used.

To reinforce the avoidant response, the threat of an adverse stimulus keeps the horse alert. Avoidance reinforcement is one of the most common forms of natural training.

Contingent: For any reinforcement to have maximum effectiveness, there must be a contingent response. Meaning this enables the horse to understand what response they are being punished.

Non-Contingent: This is a punishment that causes the horse fear, and eventually, their behavior becomes abnormal. The horse will worry more about the rider or handler's response than the task at hand.

Alternative Response: If the horse chooses the incorrect response to reinforcement, the horseman must counter with the desired response. Meaning when alternate responses are available, and the punishment is contingent on the behavior being reinforced, negative stimuli are more effective than any other type of training in causing one response to be replaced by another correct response and therefore making the negative response extinct.

The type of discipline should be chosen to limit all possibilities of abusive behaviors. No punishment that borders on abuse will obtain any positive response.

Positive Reinforcement

Primary Reinforcements: This happens when the horse learns a primary reinforcement by using natural stimuli, such as being fed. That can be used to strengthen certain behaviors; however, only a few of the primary reinforcers can be used directly for training. Although, destructive behaviors during specific times can be eliminated by reinforcing positive attitudes before the reward. Positive reinforcement training is not always apparent to many horsemen.

Natural horsemanship was developed to help eliminate the threat of horsemen using excessive negative reinforcement. During a riding session, the only reward to bestow on the horse physically is a pat on the neck or spoken word. These incentives are not naturally appreciated by the horse. The Equine responds to pressure given by stimuli such as a predator. The immediate response is movement away from the pressure applied.

Implemented: An implementation is used during a lesson when the horse chooses the correct response. An immediate release in pressure from the handler results in a positive response implemented by the horse.

Inhibition and Extinction

The intervening variable between a stimulus (functional activity) and response (result from an internal or external stimulus) is known as inhibition (restraint of behavior). The theory of inhibition is the performance of a mental task and the ability to ignore irrelevant information.

Inhibition: The influence of inhibition can be seen in horse training. When a horse is asked to perform an exercise to the left one hundred times, for example, and is then asked to repeat the exercise to the right, he will be less likely to perform equally on both sides. To balance the effects of this phenomenon, the horseman should concentrate on exercising each direction equally.

Extinction: The principle of the behavior is the ability to recognize and ignore certain acts of the horse, knowing that the horse will cease doing them. In this case, since the act was not reinforced, they will extinguish it themselves. Such behaviors might include inappropriate actions during feed times like pawing, biting, kicking, or any behavior that engages negative reinforcement by the handler.

Learning through Effects and Effort

Intelligence can be measured on many different levels. However, there is no one act of measurement to gauge the intellect of any single being. There are several ways to determine the intelligence levels of a specific animal.

Effects and Effort: The more effort that is required to learn a particular response, the harder it will be for the horse to master the response. In other words, the time and trials required to learn the response will increase as the amount of effort required increases. Natural maneuvers that evolved from being in a wild state, for example, locomotion or, more specifically, an instinctive tendency to run, do not require a lot of effort for the horse. However, teaching the horse activities, such as rollbacks, backing, or high obstacles, requires extensive amounts of effort and therefore increases the time needed to teach these maneuvers.

Shaping: A term used by behaviorists that parallels horse training in the basic foundation steps. Behavior is shaped by each successive approximation of the desired response. The importance is recognizing small responses as the horse progresses to advanced performances. For instance, the first step backward should be properly reinforced, as this will eventually lead to a good backing horse.

Fatigue: Is referred to as prolonged practice. This form of training is inefficient. During a lesson, the horse that is worked to exhaustion will learn, but at an inefficient rate. A more efficient form of training might be short practice sessions followed by brief periods of rest or simple riding.

Tasking: The horse is generally thought to perceive stimuli through the use of cues. This is proof of the horse's advanced abilities to ascertain stimuli so weak they almost cannot be perceived and was studied in the early nineteenth century by animal scientists. Horsemen should not only be able to distinguish the difference between cues given to the horse but also to use the horse's ability of tasking to promote their positive assets.

In this section of the book, not all principles of horsemanship are discussed since not all disciplines advance the learning abilities of the Equine. However, the principles that were covered attempt to develop the equestrian abilities of the horseman to a higher level of awareness.

Everlasting Stimulus

Negative reinforcement must be administered with swift, accurate precision so that it does not become an everlasting stimulus for bad behavior. If a handler inflicts punishment so severe that it causes the horse to become unmanageable, the behavior is then reinforced when cessation (complete stopping) of the punishment is stopped. Therefore, every time this particular punishment is initiated an unmanageable condition will appear. The horse's desired responses are only obtained with the knowledge to perceive the signals of the horse and the use of the correct reinforcement. Below are guidelines that explain the proper techniques to use when handling your horse to achieve desired responses.

> ➢ Learn to perceive the signals given by the horse that obtain the correct response.
> ➢ Teach the basic cues that will lead to the advancement of new cues.
> ➢ Be specific with all cues given to the horse so as not to confuse.
> ➢ Be precise with all reinforcement leading to the optimal desired response.

> Provide alternate choices when giving negative reinforcement.
> Learn to shape alternative responses caused by negative reinforcement.

For example, learning is done through positive reinforcement as the horse learns to decrease the level of negative responses.

Perfection is only achieved by patience and persistence; excess amounts of negative reinforcement will only cause abnormal behaviors, making the horse difficult to handle.

Fear instilled through excessive negative reinforcement will eliminate the progressive learning abilities of the horse.

Equines have limited reasoning abilities; expectations made above their abilities can cause abnormal behaviors.

Chapter Eleven

Ground Management

Spatial Visualization Ability

Spatial visualization is the ability to mentally manipulate two-dimensional and three-dimensional figures. This is normally measured with simple cognitive tests and is predictive of user performance with some kinds of user interfaces.

The cognitive tests used to measure spatial visualization ability include mental rotation tasks and cognitive tests like the form board, paper folding, and surface developments. Though the descriptions of spatial visualization and mental rotation sound similar, mental rotation is a particular task that can be accomplished using spatial visualization.

The Form Board: This test involves showing participants a shape and a set of smaller shapes. They are then instructed to determine which combination of smaller shapes will fill the larger shapes.

Paper Folding: This test involves showing participants a sequence of folds in a piece of paper, through which a set of holes is then punched. The participants must choose which of a set of unfolded paper with holes corresponds to the one they have just seen.

Surface Development: This test involves giving participants a flat shape with numbered sides and a three-dimensional shape with lettered sides and asks the participants to indicate which numbered side corresponds to which lettered side.

Studies have shown men have, on average, a higher standard deviation of spatial intelligence quotient than women. This domain is one of the few areas where clear sex differences in cognition appear. It also has been shown found that spatial ability correlates with verbal ability in women but not in men. This suggests that women may use different strategies for spatial visualization tasks than men.

In the past, horses were considered unintelligent, with no abstract thinking abilities, unable to generalize, and driven primarily by a herd mentality. However, recent studies show that they perform several cognitive functions daily. They frequently engage in mental challenges that include food procurement (to obtain) and social identification. They have also been shown to have a good idea of spatial discrimination abilities.

Some studies have assessed Equine intelligence in the realms of problem-solving, learning speed, and knowledge retention. Results show that horses excel at simple learning, but also can solve advanced cognitive challenges that involve categorization and concept learning. They have been shown to learn from habituation, desensitization, Pavlovian conditioning (involuntary reaction to stress or pain), and operant conditioning (the use of consequences to modify the occurrence and form of behavior). They respond to and learn from both Positive and Negative reinforcement.

Domesticated horses tend to face greater mental challenges than those of wild horses due to living in artificial environments that stifle instinctual behavior while learning tasks that are not natural. Horses are creatures of habit that respond and adapt well to regimentation and respond best when the same routines and techniques are used consistently. Some trainers believe that intelligent horses are a reflection of intelligent trainers who effectively use response conditioning techniques and positive reinforcement to train in the style that fits best with an individual animal's natural inclinations. Some who handle horses regularly note that personality also plays an important role separate from intelligence in determining how a given horse responds to various experiences.

Theories Behind Equine Management

The basic philosophy of working with horses is by appealing to their instincts and herd mentality, then extrapolate the information to adopt the closely-developed relationships that exist between horses in a natural herd environment.

The following section is written to assist the horseman with the basic ground management rules that will be used daily when handling the Equine.

Haltering the Horse

Haltering the horse properly requires two hands. The right hand is to be placed on the pole strap, and the left hand on the halter buckle. Stand on the left side of the horse between the jaw and shoulder, facing the right front side of the horse's head. Now, put the noseband of the halter over the muzzle, using the left hand to hold the halter on the horse while the right hand reaches over the horse's neck and grabs the poll strap, buckling the halter. Adjust it to fit properly, and shorten the buckle if necessary. Next, place the right hand on the lead rope about two feet from the snap, and use the left hand to carry the extra lead rope.

The excess lead should never be wrapped around the handler's hand: In the event, the horse pulls away, serious injury could be caused to the handler's hand and arm. Leading a horse may seem like a simple task for many horsemen, but there are a few rules to follow:

Lead the horse in the direction in which the handler chooses to proceed.

The handler should walk at the horse's shoulder, leaving approximately two feet between the halter and the handler's hand on the lead rope.

When entering an enclosed housing area with a horse, lead them through the entrance and make a complete circle to again face the gate before removing the halter. In this case, if the horse chooses to bolt out the gate or kick out as they run off, the handler has the option to safely escape out the entrance.

In situations where a horse must be held for a veterinarian or farrier, for example, safety mandates both people should stand on one side of the horse at all times. Every horse survives on the ability to flee dangerous situations. Particular circumstances do not change the horse's thought patterns. Contrary to popular belief, most horses will relax in moments where fear exists if an escape route is available. This also limits the risk of both or one person being injured by a fearful horse. Attempting to restrain a scared horse will only result in instilling additional fear in the persons involved in the situation.

Catching

Any horsemen's initial response to catching a difficult horse should first be deciphering the situation that caused the engagement of the flight mechanism. Usual conditions include abuse, which in normal circumstances causes stress to the horse, and the fear of experiencing the unwarranted trauma again evokes a response of flight. Remember, any object of fear will elicit fleeing the situation from the horse. The second main cause is being chased by the handler, which initiates a gameplay with the horse. In this case, the idea of running became fun. There are several things to consider when eliminating the problem, for example:

- ➢ Grain or treats must never be used as bribes.
- ➢ Avoid chasing the horse, especially in a large area.
- ➢ House the horse in a small housing environment until the problem is resolved.
- ➢ Avoid handling the horse during feeding time.

When entering the horse's housing environment, do not attempt to hide or conceal the halter and lead rope. Attention should be on completing the task at hand: catching the horse. Any deviation will be duly noted by the student. Before the process is started, ample time needs to be set aside to finish the lesson. The basic goal is catching the horse, no matter how long it takes or the effort necessary to finish the task.

Entering the housing environment, the first reaction by the student is to run off as far away as possible. Follow slowly behind so as not to start a chase; just continue with a steady, determined walk. If the horse continues to run, persist in walking towards him and just follow wherever they may go. At which point the horse chooses to stop, halt your pace. Do not attempt to move forward with the lesson until the horse has made its decision. Follow this procedure until the horse obliges to being haltered. Be patient, and remember that once a problem such as this is learned by the horse, the solution will take time to resolve. However, to remedy the problem, as with any problem, the handler must be consistent.

Reminder: Horses associate fear with objects and people, not environments.

Tying the Horse

Complications from tying have resulted in severe injury to the horse and handler.

Knots: The two basic essential knots used to tie a horse are the quick release and the escape-proof. (Note: the top rope is used as the horse's halter.)

The Quick Release is best used for a horse that does not tie well because they fidget or pull back.

The Escape Proof is best used for a horse that is mouthy and chews or plays with the lead rope. It is recommended horses be tied to an equestrian-designed hitching post, horse trailer, or cross ties. Never tie a horse to fence posts, fence rails, or fences. Injury can result from being cast in the fence or gored by the fence posts.

Grooming the Horse

Grooming is used to remove all debris from the horse's body for the placement of the saddle, cinch, bridle, and tack accessories. The horse's appearance is mainly for the horse's owner. Proper directions are as follows:

The curry is used in a circular motion, covering the entire body of the horse, excluding the legs. A soft cloth is best used with water for their legs and brush on their head and forelock.

The brush is then used to brush the entire body to remove the excess dirt brought to the surface by the curry comb. Brush in the same direction the horse's hair flows.

Comb the mane and tail using a comb or brush, starting at the bottom and working to the top.

Shampooing over a prolonged period diminishes the natural oils and dulls the coat. To bestow the horse's natural beauty in its hair coat, use a cloth diaper and rub in a circular fashion, bringing the oils to the surface.

Cleaning the Horse's Hooves

Check the horse's feet for unwanted debris regularly. Unless the horse has a thrush problem, daily cleaning is not necessary. When they are housed in a dry environment and maintained in a barefoot state, the foreign material in their feet is used as cushioning. Check for any unwanted foreign materials such as nails, wire, metal, rocks, etc. Leave the other soft material in the foot for padding.

Horses with shoes will retain material due to the horseshoe and should be cleaned regularly.

To clean the horse's foot, stand at the left or right shoulder. Facing toward the horse's tail, slide the left or right hand down the back of the leg to the fetlock and pick up the horse's foot. Hold the foot with the hand touching the horse (for the left side, use the right hand, and vice versa). Hold the foot with a cupped hand around the hoof. Place the hoof pick in the grooves of the frog to remove debris stuck in the foot. After the foot is clean, set the hoof down so as not to injure the horse by dropping the foot on the hard ground. Continue with all four, one at a time, following the same process on each foot.

Choosing a Bit

When choosing the proper bit, weigh the horse's training level in four categories.

Level One: Snaffles are recommended for level one horses. They apply intermittent pressure to the bars, but most of the pressure is still applied to the tongue. The snaffle has rings that the reins and bridle attach to. Some snaffles have hooks and/or independent side movement.

- ➢ A young green horse that has up to 30 days of riding.
- ➢ Does the horse know their gaits and basic reining, stopping, and backing?
- ➢ Does the horse give to pressure when direct pressure is applied to the rein?

Level Two: Bits with mild curbs and shanks are best for level two horses. Level two bits begin to release the tongue and add pressure to the bars of the mouth. Mild curbs may also have hooks or independent side movement.

- ➢ The horse has accomplished level one training steps.
- ➢ Does the horse relax when asked to give to pressure by holding its head position in a collected state?
- ➢ The horse should be performing more advanced gait activities, such as flying lead changes, smooth gait transformations, and stopping with the hind quarters collected.

Level Three: For level three, bits have curbs and shanks of varying lengths. Apply pressure to the bars only, along with points of the head such as the chin, poll, and palate. Independent side movement is also available.

- ➢ The horse is considered finished, and obeys cues given.
- ➢ The horse should be relaxed at the poll.
- ➢ The horse works off of the rider's seat and legs.
- ➢ Level Four is correctional bits, use for specific training problems.
- ➢ Bridling the Horse

Taking the bridle by the crownpiece, place the right hand over the horse's poll.

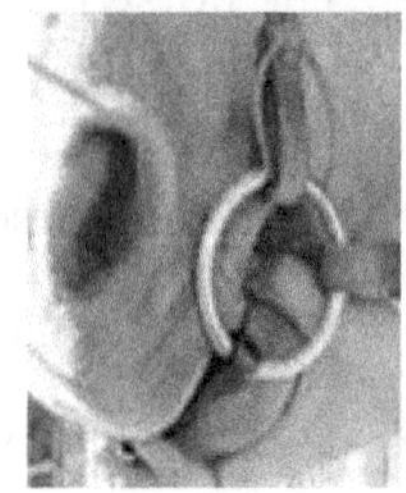

Using the thumb, open the horse's mouth, gently bringing the bit in place.

Saddling the Horse

Once grooming is completed and the horse is clean and dry of any debris, center the blanket on the horse's back about one inch in front of the horse's hip bone. The saddle should be picked up using the left hand on the saddle horn and the right hand on the cantle. Align the saddle with the cinch approximately four inches behind the horse's elbow. Next, walk to the right side of the horse and pull down the cinch, stirrup, and other attachments, such as the rear cinch or breast collar. The cinch is then tightened using the leather or nylon latigo attached to the saddle and dee rings. Cinches can be tightened using a buckle or tied, similar to a man's necktie. Using the four index fingers, there should be enough room to slide between the cinch and the horse's side snugly. Once the main cinch is attached firmly, the rest of the attachments may be connected safely. To properly saddle the horse, the main cinch is tightened first, then attach the rear cinch and breast collar. When unsaddling the horse, the rear cinch is unhooked first, then the breast collar, and finally, the main cinch.

Adjusting the Stirrups

Modern stirrups are made from a variety of materials, including wood, metal, leather, rawhide, and synthetics. When choosing a stirrup for the saddle, safety requires there to be a one-inch gap on all sides of the foot once placed in the stirrup. Widths vary according to the activity for which the saddle was designed.

Wider stirrups are generally found in events such as roping, cutting, ranch work, and trail riding. The wider stirrup tends to provide more comfort for the rider and increases stability for the foot.

Narrow stirrups are generally found in timed speed events such as barrel racing. They provide a lighter-weight saddle and less hindrance to the rider when competing in a chosen event.

Proper placement for the foot in the stirrup is on the ball, allowing the heel to fall downward and eliminating concussion to the ankle and leg of the rider. A common fault is placing the whole foot into the stirrup, putting pressure on the arch. This is a weaker position because it eliminates the flexibility of the ankle, leading to added stiffness in the knee and therefore limiting the shock-absorbency of the rider. This placement is counterproductive and should be avoided, instead, adjust the length of the stirrups.

Extend the arm with the fingertips touching the top end of the fender, under the saddle skirting. Place the stirrup under the arm, and once it reaches the armpit of the rider, the stirrup is approximately the correct length. Longer stirrups will allow for more control of the body and horse. Shorter stirrups allow the rider better movement. On average, most riders find a longer stirrup to be more comfortable, although the stirrups can be adjusted with the events the rider is participating in.

Chapter Twelve

The Fine Art of Equitation

Taking a Seat

"I do not approve of a seat which is as though the man were on a chair, but rather as though he were standing upright with his legs apart. Thus, he would get a better grip with his thighs on the horse, and being upright, he could hurl his javelin more vigorously and strike a better blow for on horseback." This statement was written by Xenophon in 350B.C., one of the great masters of equestrianism.

Equitation

The skill and theory of riding the Equine is the understanding of equitation, a primary factor to learning the art of horsemanship. The lessons written in the next section apply to both English and Western styles of riding. Basic initial skills of equitation are the same regardless of the discipline.

Horses move with the ultimate grace and agility; therefore, an improperly balanced rider will cause extreme complications for the horse. This includes behavioral problems that are simply attributed to the poor riding habits of a rider.

The rider's body must form a perpendicular line with the head, shoulders, and hips. The heels then become the adjustment point. The vertical line allows the hips to rotate forward, enabling the rider to sit on the pelvic bones. The lower body from the leg to the knee will be loose and free to move, allowing the upper thigh muscles to hold the rider in the saddle. A rider's arms remain close to the body with the chin in a level position, allowing the field of vision to focus between the horse's ears.

The reins should be held in direct line with the saddle horn. Riders can ride either with one hand or two. Keeping the wrist straight and relaxed, all four fingers should be around the reins, using the thumbs to maintain a consistent length. The rider's knuckles are turned upright toward the sky, using the ring and pinky fingers to retain contact with the horse's mouth. Contact should not be so tight that it forces the horse to gape at the mouth or toss its head. This eventually leads to a horse that refuses the bit.

Balance of the Rider

Proper balance uses the balls of the feet. With the weight of the rider's body dropping into the heels, the ankles flex downward, becoming the shock absorbers and increasing the stability of the lower leg. Turning the toes slightly outward keeps the inner calf muscle free from contact with the horse's ribcage, enabling the rider to maintain the ability to give specific cues to the horse. The knee is bent slightly to help absorb concussion and aid in gripping the saddle, along with the main gripping action by the inner thighs.

Once the horse is in motion, to maintain balance, the hip joints should be relaxed and mobile. This allows for adjustments in speed and direction changes of the horse. The rider's back is kept in a straight line, except for the small of their back, where there will be a slight arch. Keep the shoulders erect and adjacent to each other, allowing the rider to stay in the horse's center of gravity.

Depending on the amount of time you have to practice and if you have any professional guidance, learning to ride with proper equitation will vary tremendously with each person. If the rider is a beginner horseman, start with slow speeds such as a walk or jog. Do not attempt a canter, lope, or run until you have achieved proper balance at the slow speeds first.

Mounting the Horse

Before mounting the horse, always check the cinch for tightness. Some horses may blow up with air when cinching and exhale after, leaving the cinch loose. If the saddle slides more than an inch or two, the cinch should be checked for tightness. All saddles slide a small amount. The physical conditions of the rider may result in the use of a mounting block.

The reins should be in the left hand with enough tension to retain the horse's position, but not so tight it forces the horse to move. Place the right hand on the cantle and the left hand on either the saddle horn or the neck of the horse. Stand at an angle, facing the right front of the horse's head, place the left leg in the stirrup, bend the right knee slightly, and use the thigh muscle to push to a standing position. Once standing in the stirrup, swing the right leg over the horse gently and sit in the saddle. If you have trouble mounting and need to use a step, it is advisable to have someone hold the horse while mounting for added safety. Once in the saddle, check the length of the stirrups, and dismount to make adjustments when necessary.

Learning Basic Equitation Skills

Basic learning equitation skills are a necessity for becoming an accomplished rider. There are several steps involved in learning these basic lessons. First, the rider must have a flat, dry area safe to exercise the horse.

Novice horsemen start with slow speeds such as a walk or jog. Do not attempt a canter, lope, or run until you have achieved proper balance at these speeds first.

Begin at a walk, using both hands on the reins. Attempt to make a figure 8 approximately twenty feet in diameter (painting the circles on the ground is a useful tool). After accomplishing the figure 8 at a walk, begin making them at a jog or slow trot.   The lesson will help the rider achieve proper rein control of the horse. Circles, barrels, or poles can also be useful tools.

Rein control is one of the key ingredients to proper equation. The use of two hands during these lessons teaches the rider to ride in the horse's center of gravity. Equitation must be the key factor when riding a horse; this point cannot be stressed enough. Improper equation causes the majority of human injuries while participating in equestrian activities.

Caution must be taken to work the horse equally in both directions, left and right.

Collection

Collection is when a horse carries more weight on its hind legs than its front legs. When a horse draws the body in upon itself, it becomes a giant organic spring whose stored energy can be reclaimed for fighting or running from predators. The spine and associated muscles draw together in much the same action as a bow is drawn by an archer. There are two categories involved in the Equine's gait: One is *collection,* and the second is *impulsion.*

Collection in the Wild Horse

Collection is an intricate factor in the mechanism for survival. When danger suddenly appears, the horse has a large store of energy ready for instantaneous release, which

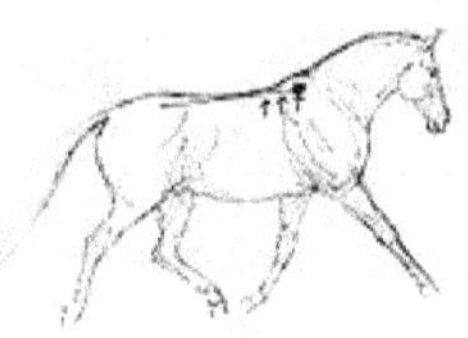

makes fleeing from danger easy and better than being caught flat-footed (on the forehand).

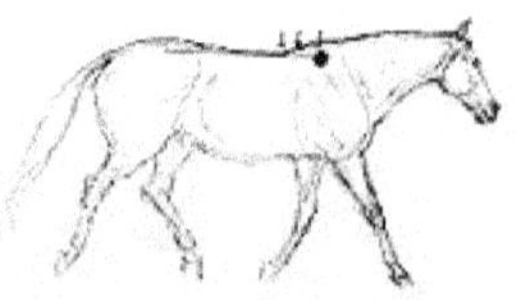

Once danger is suspected, the horse raises its head. In doing so, the back arches and the hind legs are brought under the body, where they maintain the bending of the spine with their contact with the earth. As each step is taken forward, the spring is released and then recompressed as another foot comes back under the body.

Collection in Riding

To compete in more advanced activities, collection becomes an important factor for any horseman. It not only allows the horse to move with more suppleness and increases its athletic abilities, but it also reduces wear and tear on the front legs.

The most apparent way to decipher the degree of collection as a horse travels is through a single gait. The following actions will take place.

The horse will drop their head to a level position that is aligned with the withers. This is followed by lowering the hindquarters, meaning the length of stride behind the horse will shorten, causing them to extend the stride underneath its body. This adds fluidity to the gait.

Impulsion in Riding

Impulsion is the pushing power (thrust) of the horse. This comes from their desire to move powerfully forward with the use of stored energy. However, speed will not create impulsion; a rushing horse tends to be flat rather than impulsive. The only way for a horse to have impulsion is if the hindquarters are engaged, and its elastic back allows the power to come through the movement.

A light, elastic, and expressive gait is the appearance of impulsion. To achieve impulsion, the horse needs to be forward yet relaxed and correctly collected on the bit. This means the back arches as the legs are drawn under the horse's body. The only gaits that impulsion can occur in are the trot or canter because it is found in the moment of suspension in these two gaits. To further understand the use

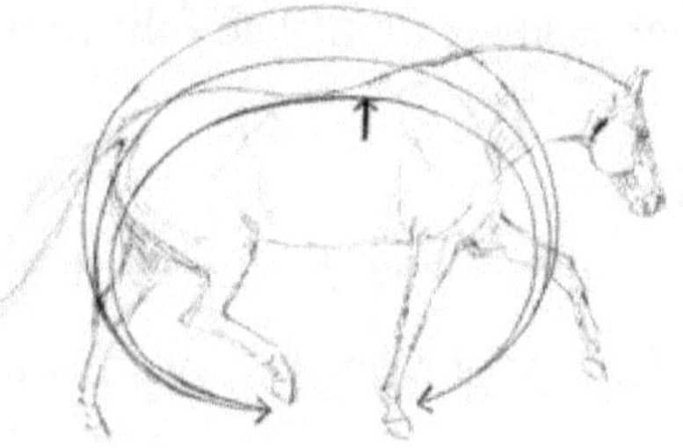

of impulsion, learning and studying the movements of dressage are recommended.

Terrestrial Locomotion

Terrestrial Locomotion (belonging to the land, rather than the sea or air) Movement on land raises different problems than that in water, with reduced friction being replaced by the effects of gravity. There are three forms of locomotion found among terrestrial animals: legged, limbless, and rolling. The Equine falls into the legged family specifically known as the unguligrade, walking on the tips of their toes.

This even further increased the length of their stride and thus speed.

The Equine Gait

Each breed of horse has its own inherited ways of travel, called gaits. Gaits are the direct evolutionary traits developed by the Equine over the last sixty million years. There are four primary or "natural" gaits for every horse: walk, trot, lope (canter), and gallop. In some breeds, the trot will be replaced by the pace or an ambling gait. However, some gaits, such as the "amble," are only performed by certain breeds of horses. Usually, the gait is natural to the breed but may require specialized training to engage the gait. The following section describes the different gaits of the Equine.

Walk: The walk has a regular cadence of 1-2-3-4, and the feet follow in sequence; left hind leg, left front leg, right hind leg, and right front leg. The horse can travel at the speed of three or four miles an hour. There is always one foot off the ground at a time, with a slight up and down movement of the head to keep their balance. For ideal travel, the advancing foot oversteps the spot where the previous foot touched the ground. The longer the horse's stride, the more comfortable the ride. All breeds have variations in the smoothness of their walk, and the rider will almost always feel some side-to-side motion. If a horse loses its regular cadence, they are most likely beginning a trot, or beginning an ambling gait.

Trot: This is a two-beat gait where the diagonal pairs of legs move in unison with each other. In the Western show horse, the slow trot is referred to as the "jog." The Standardbred horse can travel faster than the average horse can gallop, excluding the Thoroughbred racehorse.

A trot is a very stable gait for the horse, and they don't need to make any major balancing motions with the head or neck. However, it will vary dramatically in smoothness according to each horse. During the trot, it can be difficult to sit in the saddle without being bounced around because the horse drops a bit between beats, then bounces up again as the next set of legs strikes the ground. An inexperienced rider must learn specific skills to sit the trot correctly without causing injury to the horse's back.

In 1892, photographer Leland Stanford was responsible for capturing the first high-speed photo. The photo taken was of a horse fully airborne at a trot. This settled an argument about whether or not the horse became airborne at a trot.

In classic dressage, horses are asked to perform two variations of the trot, which are the "Piaffe" and the "Passage."

The Piaffe is essentially created by asking the horse to trot in place with little forward motion.

The Passage is an exaggerated slow-motion trot. Both variations of this gait require tremendous skill by the horse and rider, as well as collection by the horse.

Lope: The lope is a controlled, three-beat gait. It is slower than the gallop and the canter.

In the lope or canter, one of the horse's rear legs (for example, the right leg) propels the horse forward. During this beat, the horse is supported only on that single leg while the remaining three legs are moving forward. On the next beat, the horse catches itself on the left rear leg and right front leg, and the other hind leg is still momentarily on the ground. Then on the third beat, the horse again catches itself on the left front leg while the diagonal pair is momentarily still in contact with the ground.

Choosing a Lead

The term lead refers to the more extended foreleg that is matched by the slightly extended hind leg on the same side. The horse's lead becomes apparent when a rider is put into the equation. It changes not only the horse's balance but also its center of gravity. As the rider performs activities on the horse, it usually happens in an enclosed area, for instance, a round pen or arena. To maintain the horse's natural balance, they must be on the lead that follows the direction in which the horse is traveling: left direction, left lead, right direction, right lead.

The Equine has impeccable agility that allows them to change from one lead to the next with every beat of the lope. For example, a pole-bending horse will change leads with every bend through the poles. Jumping horses will land from a jump on the lead approaching the next turn and jump. Performance horses like barrel racing horses, rope horses, cutting horses, or reining horses all require the horse to perform what is known as the "flying" lead change. A flying lead change requires the horse to switch from one lead to the next in a straight line.

Gallop: The gallop is similar to the lope, except faster and covers more ground. However, the third stage of the lope is a three-beat gait, while the gallop is the fastest four-beat gait. Like the lope, the horse will strike off with its non-leading hind foot, but the second stage of the lope becomes, in the gallop, the second and third stages because the inside hind foot hits the ground a split second before the outside front foot. Then both gaits end with the striking off of the leading leg, followed by a moment of suspension when all four feet are off the ground.

There are classic paintings of racehorses depicted with all four legs stretched out at this stage of the gallop; in actuality, all four feet of the horse are off the ground and bent inward, not stretched out. An average horse can gallop twenty-five to thirty mph. This allows them to cover short distances quickly, but they will seldom continue these high rates of speed for more than a mile or two.

The Thoroughbred is classically seen in photographs at a gallop. As a colt, Secretariat had an average stride of 24.6 feet, extending to the distance of 24.8 feet as an adult. This is most likely the major factor in his success, along with the increased size of his heart.

Most racehorses do not run longer than a mile and a half. However, Arabians have raced as far as two to three and a half miles. Quarter Horses achieved their fame as racehorses due to their ability to reach speeds of fifty-five miles per hour at the quarter of a mile.

Finally, the last of the natural gaits is the "pace"; however, not all breeds can perform the pace.

Pace: The pace is a lateral ,two-beat gait in which the two legs on the same side move forward together in unison.

As a rule, the pace is extremely uncomfortable to ride and next to impossible to sit, nor is posting an option. Another natural pacer is the camel. Due to the fact the camel is much faster and can move at greater speeds, in one reason the riders can follow the rocking motion.

The Icelandic horse's pace is called "skeio, " which is a highly desirable gait that is ridden for short distances at quick speeds, known as the "flugskeio`" or flying pace.

The Peruvian Paso has a gait somewhat between the pace and amble, called the "sobreandando." Pacing horses that are not used for harness are often taught to perform some form of amble, which requires the horse to maintain a slightly unbalanced footfall. This breaks the pace into a four beat lateral gait, allowing for a smoother ride.

Ambling Gaits

Today, especially in the United States, horses that can perform more than three gaits are referred to as "gaited" horses. In the past, all the gaits we grouped and called the ambling gaits. All the ambling gaits are faster than a walk, but slower than a canter, and can be maintained by the horse for long periods, such as the Tennessee Walker.

There are two basic types of amble gaits, the first being lateral, wherein the front and hind feet on the same side move in sequence. The second is diagonal, where the front and hind feet of the opposite side move in sequence. Only a few horses can naturally perform all the ambling gaits; for example, several breeds inherit the ability to perform the gaits either at birth or with minimal training. The six ambling gaits are listed below.

The Fox Trot was first associated with the Missouri Fox Trotter but is now common in other breeds. This is a four-beat diagonal gait in which the front foot of the diagonal pair lands before the hind.

The Paso Gaits are only characteristic of the Peruvian Paso and the Paso Fino. The Paso Gait includes a range of smooth intermediate lateral ambling gaits, from slow to fast: the paso fino, paso corto, paso largo. The termino is characteristic of the Peruvian Paso, which is an elongated lateral motion of the front shoulder.

The Rack is associated with the American Saddlebred, which is true five-gaited horses. This four-beat gait has an equal interval between each beat. Saddlebreds can only perform the rack for short periods of time due to the amount of agility and stamina needed to perform the gait.

The Running Walk is also a four-beat lateral gait with the footfalls in the same sequence as the regular walk but characterized by greater speed and comfort. It is a distinctive gait of the Tennessee Walker.

The Slow Gait is a general term for several slightly different gaits. The gait follows the same footfall pattern, as the lateral pairs of legs move forward in the sequence, but the rhythm and collection of the movements are different. Common terms for slow gaits are the stepping pace and the singlefoot.

The Tolt is unique to the Icelandic Horse. In its pure form, the footfall is the same pattern as the rack, but the Icelandic Horse is bred for more freedom and liquidity of movement.

Chapter Thirteen

Buying a Horse

The Horse

The words written in this chapter are based on the knowledge acquired by the famous horsemen who thought as I do.

The Equine is a magical creature that can make little girls cry; men gleam with pride and women who need a friendly smile. My goal for this handbook is to clear--- whatever, has been missed in many previous treatises.

To begin this chapter, a list of suggestions is given to provide information that will help eliminate being cheated when purchasing a horse.

For the potential horse owner, a literary statement comes to mind, written by the Father Almighty, for the sole purpose of reminding humans why horses are present on Earth:

"The horse was brought to man by the sacred hand of God, for the sole purpose, of enlightening our lives with joy, peace, and honor."

How to Approach Buying a Horse

To begin the decision to purchase a horse, the potential owner must first know the basic breeds of Equine and equestrian activities to participate in. Once these choices have been made, the buyer can proceed in finding the best horse to suit the individual's needs.

Original Wild Prototypes

There are four original wild prototypes (the original model) from which domestic breeds developed.

- ➤ Warmblood subspecies or forest horse (Equus ferus silvaticus)
- ➤ Oriental subspecies (Equus agilis)
- ➤ Draft subspecies
- ➤ Tarpan subspecies

Common Breeds of the Equine

The Barb is known as the desert horse; however, due to the amount of cross-breeding, it is difficult to find a pure-bred Barb today. Nevertheless, the Barb has had an incredible impact on today's modern breeds. The exact development of the breed is unknown, but it originated on the Barbary Coast of North Africa during the eighth century, about the same time the Islamic invaders reached the region. There has been controversy over the idea of whether the Barb and Arabians come from the same bloodline or different ancestry.

When the Barb was imported to Europe, they were sometimes mistaken for Arabians due to the fact the horse handlers were African Muslims who only spoke Arabic. This means there is a good chance the Godolphin Arabian may have been mistaken for a Barb stallion.

Today there are several varieties of the Barb, including the Algerian, Moroccan, and Tunisian. Although it is unlikely the true origin of this breed will ever be revealed, one thing is for certain: The Barb's influence can be seen in modern-day breeds such as the American Quarter Horse, the Mustang, and the Appaloosa. Despite their influence as a progenitor of other breeds, the Barb has not achieved widespread fame like the Arabian, no doubt because it lacks the same visual appeal. The Barb is much less defined and generally less impressive in appearance. However, they carry the same ability to thrive on meager rations; they are sure-footed, have an impressive turn of speed over short distances, good gaits, and boundless stamina. The Barb stands between 13.3 hands to 14.1 hands and ranges from gray, bay, black, chestnut, and brown. To preserve the breed, the World Barb Organization was founded in 1987 and is based in Algeria. However, because of political situations, it is difficult to predict the breed's outcome for retaining its purity.

The Mustang is a free-roaming feral horse in western North America. In 1971, the United States Congress recognized Mustangs as living symbols of the historic and pioneer spirit of the West. Their presence contributes to the diversity of horses and enriches the lives of the people today.

The original Mustang descended from Iberian horses brought to Mexico and Florida by the Spanish. Most of these horses were of Andalusian, Arabian, and Barb ancestry. Starting in the colonial era and continuing with the westward expansion of the 1800s, some ranchers attempted to "improve" the Mustang breed by shooting the dominant stallion and replacing them with pedigreed animals. By the 1900s, North America had an estimated two million free-roaming horses; since then, the Mustang population has reduced dramatically due to capture by hunters, military use, and slaughter for food, especially dog food. Since then, the free-roaming horse protection law was enacted in 1959. The Bureau of Land Management is tasked with protecting, managing, and controlling wild horses and burros.

Today, free-roaming horses have disappeared from six states, and their populations are fewer than twenty-five thousand. More than half of them are in Nevada; the remaining population resides in Montana and Oregon. A few hundred survive in Alberta and British Columbia. The Mustang is a free-roaming feral horse that has had a major influence on our society and not only the horse world but also the movie industry and tourism. Therefore, maintaining the safety and well-being of one of the most beloved icons in American history is essential.

The Arabian (AHRA) has a history that is clouded by controversy. However, the foundation stock for this breed has existed for 4,500 hundred years in the mid-east and northern deserts of the Arabian Peninsula. Some historians believe the Barb horses of northern Africa were the ancestors of the Arabian, although some believe the Arabians were used for breeding the Barb.

Almost every breed of riding horse in the world can be traced to the Arabian. However, even with their long ancestry, the Arabian registry did not come about until 1908. As a matter of fact, they were not even imported into America until the Revolutionary War when Homer Davenport imported 27 horses from the Arabian Desert, which spared the organization of the breed. The initial registry included seventy-one horses, and by the end of 1973, one hundred thousand horses were registered.

American colonists Nathaniel Harrison imported horses of Arabian, Barb, and Turkish ancestry to America in 1747. These two horses were ridden by George Washington during the Revolutionary War. Their names were "Blueskin," and the other was a stallion named "Ranger." Presidents Van Buren and Ulysses S. Grant obtained two Arabian stallions as a diplomatic gift from the Sultan of Turkey. Both of these horses were bred with other horses and appear in the pedigrees today, such as the Appaloosa horse.

Regardless of origins, climates, and culture ultimately created the Arabian. Living in a desert environment required domesticated horses to cooperate with humans for survival. They were the only providers of food and water in certain areas. Even the hardy Arabian horse needed far more water than camels to survive (most horses can only survive about 72 hours without water). Desert horses were fed dates and camel's milk. Furthermore, they must possess anatomical traits to adapt to life in a dry climate along with wide temperature extremes from day to night. In other words, only the strongest survived.

Owing to this close relationship with humans, Arabians were bred to be war horses, so speed, endurance, soundness, and intelligence were a necessity. Many raids required stealth, and mares were preferred over stallions due to the fact they were quieter and did not give the soldiers' position away.

The average size of the Arabian is 14.1 hands to 15.1 hands, with their weight varying from 800 to 1000 pounds. The recognized color coats in purebred are bay, gray, chestnut, black, and roan. One of the most distinctive features of the Arabian is the "dished" profile. Many Arabians have a slight forehead bulge between their eyes, called a "jibba." That adds additional sinus capacity, which is believed to increase stamina in desert climates. This breed also has a long-arched neck, large wide-set eyes, level croup, and a naturally high tail carriage. Well-bred Arabians have deep, well-angled hips, laid-back shoulders, and short backs. Some, but not all, have five lumbar vertebrae instead of the usual six. There are also seventeen rather than eighteen pairs of ribs. Thus, most Arabians usually possess dense, strong bones, sound feet, and good hoof walls, and are especially noted for endurance.

The Arabian horse is one of many breeds that is very high-spirited and intelligent; therefore, they are not always suited for the beginner rider. For novice horsemen who already own Arabians, guidance from an equestrian professional may be necessary.

The Appaloosa (ApHC) was originally developed by the Nez Perce' in the American Pacific Northwest, on the "Palouse River." The earliest evidence of horses with spotted coat patterns was found in Lascaux and Peche-Merle in France, dating back to the Upper Paleolithic era circa 18,000 B.C. Other evidence of cave art has been found in Persia, Ancient Greece, the Tang Dynasty of China, and eleventh-century France.

Historians are not sure how the spotted horse arrived in the Americas, but they know the Appaloosa had reached the Pacific Northwest by the 1700s. The Nez Perce people were known to be notable breeders in the early 1800s.

Lewis and Clark documented that the early Nez Perce' were considered to have bred horses of high quality. They stated in a journal entry on February 15, 1806, "The horses appear to be of an excellent race; they are lofty, elegantly formed, active, and durable: in short many of them look like fine English horses, and would make a figure of any country."

Noted down in further detail were statements made about coat patterns, calling them "pided," with some large spots of white irregularly scattered and intermixed with brown, black, bay, or some other dark colors. The term "pided" is believed to mean "pinto." However, some historians argue that only ten percent of the Nez Perce's horses were spotted at the time. It wasn't until after the arrival of Lewis and Clark that color was emphasized in breeding programs. The Nez Perce' was a peaceful nation and engaged in agriculture and horse breeding.

When the gold miners settled in the1860s, they put pressure on the tribe, forcing them to give up seven million acres due to the treaties between 1855 and 1863. After the capture of Chief Joseph, the Appaloosa horse nearly disappeared. However, it was not until 1938 that the Appaloosa Horse Registry was formed, and they hoped to preserve, improve, and standardize the breed to the original guidelines. A horse with endurance, surefootedness, and hardy range animal.

The Appaloosa has a smooth, elegant muscle formation. The base colors accepted by the ApHc are bay, black, chestnut, palomino, buckskin, dun, and grulla, although the unique color patterns are the distinguishing factors of the Appaloosa horse.

Recognized spotting patterns include:

Blanket is a white cover over the hip that may extend from the tail to the base of the neck. The spots inside the blanket (if present) are the same color as the horse's base coat.

Leopard has white patterning that is exhibited to an extreme, with the base colored spots of various sizes covering most of the body.

Few Spot Leopard has the horse's base color nearly obscured by its Appaloosa white patterning, covering up to ninety percent of the body. The horse may exhibit patches of color on the head, knees, elbows, and flanks (called vanish marks). Some may have as few as one or two spots.

A horse with white spots or flecks on a dark body is known as Snowflake. Typically, the white spots increase in number and size as the horse ages.

Varnish has dark points (legs and head) and some spots or roaning over a light body. This may occur in conjunction with another spotting style and change with age. It often starts as a solid-colored horse that gets withered as it ages but is not gray.

Frost is similar to varnish, but the white hairs are limited to the back, loins, and neck. It may occur in conjunction with another spotting style and change with age. It often starts as a solid-colored horse that will get additional white with age.

To obtain a regular registration, the horse must also exhibit certain other characteristics, which are discussed below.

Mottling Spotted Skin, which is apparent around the lips, eyelids, and genitalia. The Appaloosa is the only horse to have this characteristic. Therefore, mottled skin is a very basic and decisive indication of an Appaloosa. Mottled skin is different from pink skin in that it will normally contain small, round, dark spots of pigmented skin.

Sclera is a white ring around the eye.

Stripped hooves are white and black stripes down the hoof from the cornet band to the bottom of the hoof wall.

Although most Appaloosas are recognized for their colorful spotted coat patterns, striped hooves, and mottled skin, they can also have several eye colors, such as brown, hazel, and blue. On occasion, Appaloosas are known to have different colored eyes. The breed characteristic is coat color patterns, not body conformation, making the Appaloosa a versatile horse for any equestrian activity. Other popular spotted horse breeds are the Pony of America, the Colorado Ranger, and the Tiger Horse.

The Appaloosa is not just a color breed, as sometimes thought. All ApHC registered horses must be offspring of two registered Appaloosa parents or approved breeds such as Arabian, Quarter Horses, and Thoroughbreds. Therefore, the typical build, height, and weight will vary from one horse to the next. Appaloosas are noted for their calm, even-tempered nature and all-around versatility.

The American Quarter Horse (AQHA) was developed in the 1600s when the American colonists on the Eastern Seaboard began to cross the English Thoroughbred with assorted native horses such as the Chickasaw, a horse breed by the Native American people descending from Spain. In 1746, a foal was born by the name of Janus, who contributed crucial genes in the development of the "Quarter Miler."

The average Quarter Horse can reach speeds of fifty-five mph. This line of breeding resulted in a small, hardy, quick, and useful workhorse that could run cattle all week and compete in weekend match races. The early foundation sires were Quarter Horses such as Steel Dust, foaled in 1843, Shiloh, foaled in 1844; and Old Cold Deck, foaled in 1862. These are just a few of the old-timers.

In 1940, the American Quarter Horse Association was formed, and the first registration went to the honored P-1 Wimpy, a descendant of the King Ranch, the foundation sire of Old Sorrel. The only Thoroughbred stallion that has the honor of being recognized by the AQHA Hall of Fame is Three Bars. The Quarter Horse ranges from 14 hands to 16 hands, with a well-muscled, straight profile, and is best known for their lightning speeds in a quarter mile, quick, agile movements, and very powerful hindquarters while working cattle. Their average weight is 1200 pounds, and they are found in the common colors: sorrel, bay, black, buckskin, palomino, gray, dun, red dun, grullo, red roan, blue roan, bay roan, perlino, and cremello. Current registration of the Quarter Horse requires DNA testing of the parents to verify lineage. There are over five million Quarter Horses registered in the world today. Quarter Horses are one of the most common breeds of horses found today. They are considered to be calm, intelligent, and versatile.

The Thoroughbred (The Jockey Club) was developed for
speed at intermediate distances. However, no other type of
Equine has influenced the development of the light horse
breeds like the Thoroughbred. Foundation stallions were
used to develop breeds such as the Standardbred, the
American Saddle Horse, the Morgan, and the Quarter
Horse. In fact, General George A. Custer was mounted on a
Thoroughbred at the battle of Little Big Horse River on
June 25, 1876.

The foundation sires of the Thoroughbred were:

- Byerly Turk foaled in 1679, brought to England by
  Captain Byerly in 1689.
- Herod, a great-grandson, foaled in 1758.
- Matchem was foaled in 1748.
- Eclipse was foaled in 1748, who was unbeaten in
  twenty-six starts.
- Bulle Rock is traditionally regarded as the first
  Thoroughbred imported into America in 1730 at the
  age of 21 years old.

The first registered Thoroughbred was recorded in 1791 by
James Weatherby Jr. in his "Introduction to a General Stud
Book."

In 1973, Secretariat became the first three-year-old horse in twenty-five years to win. His amazing performance was at Belmont, where he broke the track record of 2:26 3/5 by 2 3/5 seconds. However, he was only slightly dulled by the performances of the original Big Red and Man-O-War, who won twenty-one out of twenty-two starts. Although, Man-O-War never competed in the Kentucky Derby.

Thoroughbreds are noted for having a long forearm and gaskin. They display considerable length from the hip to the hock and long smooth muscles enabling them to excel at the run. The average Thoroughbred ranges from 15.1 hands to 16.2 hands, and the average weight is 900-1500 pounds. Modern Thoroughbreds are nearly two hands taller than the foundation sires. The Jockey Club recognizes black, dark bay, brown, bay, chestnut, gray and roan colors for the Thoroughbred. White is so rare that the first registered white horse was not until 1963, a filly named White Beauty. The Thoroughbred is known for speed and athletic abilities concerning racing and Grand Prix jumping. They are characterized as the English discipline performance horse.

The Morgan (MHR) is the only breed to be founded after a real horse. The foundation sire of the Morgan was a stallion named Figure. As a foal, he took the name of his owner, which was the custom. *Justin Morgan*, the horse, became famous due to his progeny that gave him the ability to out-pull, outrun, outwalk, and out trot all competition. Justin Morgan, the horse, died in 1821 at the age of twenty-one years old. He is interred in Tunbridge, Vermont.

The breed's trotting ability made them popular for harness racing in the 1840s. This continued until the Standardbred defined the meaning of throttle (maximum speed). Morgans were common in the Civil War as cavalry mounts, including Sheridan's "Rienzi" and Stonewall Jackson's "Little Sorrel." In the post-Civil War era, Morgans were particularly popular for the Pony Express riders and the cavalry in the Western United States. A little unknown fact of history is one of the only survivors of the Custer regiment from the Battle of Little Bighorn was the Morgan-Mustang horse named Comanche.

The Morgan horse registry was formed in 1894. Since then, more than 132,000 Morgan horses have been registered. The Morgan horse had a major influence on several particular breeds, like the Tennessee Walker, the American Quarter Horse, and the American Saddlebred. The breed ranges from 14.1 hands to 15.2 hands and can vary in colors from bay, black, and chestnut. Less common colors include gray, palomino, roan, cremello, perlino, dun, buckskin, and silver dapple. Three pinto colors exist today: sabino, frame overo, and splash overo. However, the tobiano pattern is not noted in the Morgan horse.

Morgan horses are compact and refined in build, with strong limbs, expressive faces, large eyes, defined withers, laid-back shoulders, and a well-arched neck. There is officially one breed standard for the Morgan horse, regardless of the discipline or bloodline of the individual animal. One of their greatest qualities is versatility, along with their ability to gait, which improves the ride.

The Tennessee Walker was bred to be gentle; this, along with their unique four-beat "running walk," makes them especially comfortable and a well-suited trail companion. In the early 1800s, two breeds, the Narragansett Pacer and the Canadian Pacer, were blended to develop a horse that could handle the mountainous terrain of the area in the Southern United States to carry the plantation owners around their land. Later, the Thoroughbred, Morgan, and American Standardbred were used to refine the bloodlines, gait, and stamina.

In 1855, Black Allen was born, and he became the foundation sire of the Tennessee Walker. The registry was formed in 1935, and the stud book was closed in 1947. Their conformation has remained consistent since then, with features including a long neck and sloping shoulders. The head is traditionally large but refined in bone, with small, well-placed ears, an elongated stride, and a long flowing mane and tail. This breed ranges from 15 hands to 17 hands and sometimes reaches 18 hands. Their weight ranges from 900 to 1200 pounds. This breed, though normally well-tempered, has an extremely long stride and moves at higher speeds, which can be intimidating to some novice riders.

The Missouri Fox Trotter (MFTHBA) came about in the early 19th century when the pioneers came to the rugged foothills of the Ozarks in Missouri, Tennessee, Virginia, and Kentucky. They soon realized that a horse with a natural four-beat gait would be ideal for the rocky and thickly forested land. Selectively bred to develop the gliding fox trot, breeders combined the bloodlines of the American Saddle Horse, Standardbred, Tennessee Walker, Morgan, Thoroughbred, and Arabian.

The four foundation stallions were:

- Brimmer, a Thoroughbred
- Old Skip, a Morgan/Thoroughbred
- Chief
- Cotham Dare

The breeders association was formed in 1948 but not recognized until 1958 as the Missouri Fox Trotter Horse Breeders' Association. The breed is best known for its unique gait, called the fox trot, in which the horse appears to walk with its front leg and trot with the hind. The four-beat motion, rather than a two-beat trot, allows the gait to be easy to sit. The trot is accompanied by an up-and-down nodding of the head; however, the gait is not followed by a high stepping action but rather a very smooth, comfortable ride. Fox Trotters can reach speeds up to ten mph. They have a gentle disposition and are surefooted. They generally stand 14.2 hands to 16.2 hands. Fox Trotter colors include common Equine colors and most pinto spotting patterns, excluding Appaloosa markings. Similar to most gaited horses, Fox Trotters have an elevated neck, head, and tail carriage, sloping shoulders, short back with a rounded croup, and a slender body with a deep chest.

The American Saddle Horse was originally bred in the United States for the bluegrass plains of Kentucky, areas of Tennessee, Virginia, West Virginia, and later Missouri. The people needed a smooth, easy-riding, general-purpose horse that could travel great distances with speed and endurance.

The American Saddle Horse can be traced to the Thoroughbred stallion Denmark, Mambrino Chief, a trotter, which traces back to the Thoroughbred Messenger. As needs changed, the American Saddle Horse developed into what is called the peacock of the horse world. A stylish, fancy horse, beautiful for harness, strong enough for farm work, fast enough for match races, and became popular after the stallion Denmark was noted as one of the foundations sires in the 1840s.

Many famous soldiers used this breed, including Generals Ulysses S Grant and Stonewall Jackson and General Robert E. Lee, who had a Saddlebred named "Traveller." Popular culture even promoted the American Saddle Horse, including the golden age of Hollywood's portrayal of "Mr. ED" and *"Flicka,"* one of the horses in National Velvet. Saddlebreds can be seen in the classic film "Gone with the Wind," and movies like the original Zorro. Even actors today own the flashy American Saddlebred, such as William Shatner, Patrick Stewart, and Carson Kressley.

The Saddlebred stands an average of 14.2 hands to 17 hands, weighs 1,000 to 1,2000 pounds, and varies in colors of black, bay, chestnut, brown, gray, buckskin, palomino, pinto, and occasionally roan. They perform five gaits, starting from the walk, trot, and canter, followed by the slow gait and rack. Most of the Saddlebreds today can learn additional gaits as well. Saddlebreds tend to be high-spirited but gentle-natured, and may not be well suited for novice riders.

Color Genetics and Color Breeds

Color Genetics

The Equine offers a diverse array of color variations and distinctive markings that are unique to each horse. Breed associations have chosen a specialized vocabulary to describe them. As a matter of fact, humans tend to notice the color of a horse before their age, breed, and sex. Most horses remain the same color throughout their lifetime; however, some may develop a different color from which they were born over several years. White markings present at birth and the underlying skin color of a horse do not change; unless disease or injury. Today, the myths of color genetics have been largely resolved. DNA testing will likely determine an offspring's color or at least give possible variations.

There is some controversy about the details of how genetics contribute to the arrangement of color patterns and white markings.

To start, each horse begins with the basic coat color; chestnut is called "red" by geneticists. This is known as the absence of the extension gene "e," or "black," based on the presence of the extension gene "E."

The initial set of genes that all other color genes act upon is the basic set. However, when at least one copy of another gene is present as the dominant allele, this creates the vast range of colors that all horses possess.

- ➢ Many classes of horses are determined by particular characteristics, not confirmation or breed. For example:
- ➢ Color
- ➢ Excessive white
- ➢ Specific colors

However, there are some true breeds of horses that have color preferences but are not color registries, such as the Friesian Horse, which is always black, or the Appaloosa, which must have specific spot patterns.

Next is the list of horses based on the primary foundation classifications of each type that preserves the breed standard. The following list starts with the most common horse colors and proceeds to the most unpredictable colors.

Body Colors

Bay: Body color ranges from a light reddish-brown to very dark brown and "black points." Points are located on the mane, tail, and lower legs. The color variations are:

Dark Bay is a very dark red or brown hair, sometimes referred to as black bay, mahogany bay, or brown bay.

Blood Bay is bright red, and shade variations are often considered simply bay.

Light Bay is more clearly red than gold.

Brown: All brown horses are either genetically bay if they carry the "E" gene or genetically chestnut if they do not. Without DNA testing, a determination can be made by looking at the mane, tail, and legs for black points.

Chestnut: A reddish body color with no black in the horse's mane and tail. The mane and tail will be some shade lighter or darker than the body color. The main color variations of chestnut are:

Liver Chestnut is a very dark brown coat.

Sorrel has a reddish tan coat, about the same as a newly minted penny.

Blond or Light Chestnut is very seldom used; however, the mane and tail are lighter than the coat but not quite a dun.

 Gray: In this case, a horse has black skin with white and dark mixed hair. Gray horses can be born any color and lighten as they age. Eventually, most will turn either completely white or "flea-bitten." Most white horses are gray with a fully white hair coat. Gray horses are distinguished from white horses by dark skin, especially around the eyes, muzzle, flanks, and other areas with no hair. Variations of gray include:

Steel Gray is common in younger horses. The horse has white and dark hairs evenly intermixed over most of the body.

Dapple Gray is a dark-colored horse with lighter rings of graying hairs, called dapples, scattered throughout the body.

Flea-Bitten Gray is an otherwise fully white-haired horse that develops red hairs flecked throughout the coat.

Rose Gray is a horse with a reddish or pinkish tinge to its coat. This color occurs when a horse born bay or chestnut "grays out" with age.

Roan: The roan horse color pattern allows the white hairs to be evenly intermixed within the horse's body color. Roan horses typically do not change color in their lifetime. The head is usually much darker and possibly solid-colored, whereas the body hair is roaned. The following are some color variations:

Red Roan is a chestnut base coat with a roan pattern, the mane and tail being the same color as the horse's body. These horses are sometimes called Strawberry Roans.

Bay Roan is a bay base coat with a roan pattern, with a black mane and tail.

Blue Roan is a black horse with roan patterns and hairs that have a blue color, not to be confused with a gray or a blue dun/grullo. Blue Roans have mixed-colored hairs.

Rabicano is a roan-like effect caused by a genetic modifier that creates a mealy, splotchy, or roan pattern on only part of the body, usually limited to the underside of the horse's, flanks, legs, tail, or head areas. Unlike a true roan, much of the body will not have white hairs intermingled with solid ones, nor are the legs significantly darker than the rest of the horse.

Uncommon Body Colors

The most unpredictable colors include:

Black: Black is relatively uncommon, though not "rare." There are two types of black, fading black and non-fading black. Most black horses will fade to a brownish color if the horse is exposed to sunlight regularly. Non-fading black is a blue-black shade that does not fade in the sun. Genetically, the two cannot yet be differentiated, and some claim the difference occurs due to management rather than genetics. Although, this claim is highly disputed. Most foals are born mousy gray or dun and shed to a black coat. For the horse to be a true black, it must be completely black except for any white markings. The difference can be seen around the eye and muzzle. A true black will have all-black hairs, while a dark chestnut will not.

Brindle: The brindle horse is one of the rarest colors. The characteristic of any color variation contains "zebra-like" stripes or primitive markings. The most common is a brown horse with faint yellowish markings.

Buckskin: Found in the bay horse with one copy of the cream gene, a dilution gene that dilutes the coat color to a yellow cream or gold while keeping the black points.

Champagne: Produced by a different dilution gene than the cream gene. It lightens both skin and hair but creates a metallic gold coat color with mottled skin and light-colored eyes. The champagne horse is often confused with palomino, cremello, dun, and buckskin horses.

Cream dilution: An incomplete dominant gene that produces a partially diluted coat color with one copy of the allele and a full dilution with two copies. This color includes palomino, buckskin, perlino, cremello, smoky cream, and smoky black.

Silver Dapple: The dilution gene acts only upon black hair pigment, lightening black body hair to a chocolate brown and the mane and tail to silver. A horse can carry the gene. The horse with a red coat will not show any visible signs.

Perlino: Similar to a cremello, but acts genetically as a bay base coat with two dilute genes. The eyes are usually blue. The mane, tail, and points are darker than the body but not black. Most likely, they will be reddish or rust color. Not to be confused with a red dun.

White: The white horse is one of the rarest colors. The mane and tail are white, with pink skin. Some have blue eyes and will remain white for life. A truly white horse occurs in one of two ways, either by inheriting one copy of the dominant white (W) gene or by being a fully expressed sabino (essentially a horse that is one big white spot). The vast majority of white horses are actually graying with a fully white hair coat.

Albino: There is no true albino in the horse world (white coat with pink skin and pink eyes). If a foal is a true albino, it will die either in the womb or shortly after birth. The Equine coat color genetics that factors into creating true albinism is not yet fully understood and lethal in horses.

Common Color Breeds of the Equine

The Palomino Horse (PHBA): A chestnut horse that has one cream dilution gene that turns the horse golden, yellow, or a tan shade, with a flaxen or white mane and tail. Palominos are often cited as being a color within three shades of a newly minted gold coin. It was originally derived from the golden grape of California, the Palomino grape. Early origins of the Palomino Horse date back to Queen Isabella of Spain and was introduced by Cortez and early Spanish explorers to the Americas. There are three distinct colors of Palomino, starting with extremely light, almost cremello, to deep chocolate. The horse must have a flaxen or white mane and tail. The breed registry was formed in 1932.

"Again, I raised my eyes, and this is what I saw: four chariots coming out between two mountains, and the mountains were mountains of bronze. The first chariot had red horses, the second chariot had black horses, the third chariot had white horses, and the fourth chariot had vigorous, piebald horses." Zechariah 5: 1, 3

The Paint Horse (APHA): The word paint, pinto, and spotted is used by three associations to describe a horse with colored spots. The word pinto comes from Spanish, meaning paint, painted, or spotted. The American Paint Horse Association was formed in 1965, giving horses born with excessive white or spotted markings registration capabilities. An APHA retains the same body style as the Quarter Horse and Thoroughbred; a muscular animal that is heavy but not too tall and has a low center of gravity for maneuverability, along with powerful hindquarters that are suitable for rapid acceleration.

To be registered, the horse must have American Quarter Horse, American Paint Horse, or Thoroughbred bloodlines. APHA will accept a small number of "solids" into the registry, with regulations (known as breeding stock). The area with white must cover a minimum span of two or more inches, and be located in certain areas of the body. The skin must be pink under the white hair. The following list is the color variations included by both Pinto and Paint registrations.

The Pinto Horse (PHAA): The Pinto Horse Association was formed in 1956. The Pinto can be any breed of horse, whereas the Paint Horse is only registered with bloodlines tracing to the American Quarter Horse, the Thoroughbred, or the Paint Horse.

Variations include:

Piehabald (UK term): A black-and-white spotting pattern.

Skewbald (UK term): A spotting pattern with white or any other color besides black. A spotting pattern of white and two other colors, which may include black.

Tobiano: A spotting pattern characterized by rounded markings and white legs. The white crosses the back, consisting of more dark than white. Normally the head is dark, with markings of a solid horse, such as a star, snip, blaze, or strip.

Overo: A spotting pattern characterized by sharp, irregular markings with a horizontal orientation, usually more white than dark. The face is more often white, with the occasional blue eyes. The white rarely crosses the black, and the lower legs will likely be dark. Variations include the Frame Overo and the Splash White.

Sabino: A light spotting pattern characterized by high white on the legs and belly spots. White markings on the face extend past the eyes, and/or patches of roan patterns stand alone or on the edges of the white markings. Often confused with the roan or rabicano (roan horse color pattern).

Tovero: A spotting pattern characterized by a mix of Tobiano and Overo coloration, such as blue eyes on a dark head or a horse with Tobiano coloring carrying a recessive Overo gene.

Medicine Hat: An uncommon pattern where the poll and ears are dark, surrounded by white. A true "medicine hat" Pinto or Paint has additional characteristics, such as the body being predominantly white, with dark coloration by the flanks and around the eyes.

Shield: A large dark patch covering the chest, surrounded by white, usually on a predominately white horse.

In recent years, the breed developed several medical issues involving genetic diseases, such as HYPP and HERDA, which some believe make them more pronged to Wobblers' Syndrome.

The Buckskin Horse (IBHA): Buckskin is a color, not a breed of horse. The Soraya and Norwegian Dun of Spain were crossed with the Barb and Arabian horses in Spain.

The Fjord horse is one of the world's oldest and purest breeds, believed to be related to the Przewalski, a primitive wild horse of Asia. Horses were known to exist in Norway at the end of the last ice age. It is believed that the ancestors of the modern Fjord horse migrated to Norway and were domesticated over 4,000 years ago. Archaeological excavations at Viking burial sites indicate that the Fjord horse type has been selectively bred for at least 2,000 years. Over the next seven hundred years, the breed was introduced to Mexico and the United States by Spanish explorers in the early sixteenth century. They are unlike the Dun horse that carries the dun gene; the buckskin horse carries the crème gene; although, they can carry both genes and are called "dunskins." Any primitive striping beyond the dorsal stripe are remnant of the dun gene. Buckskin occurs as a result of the cream dilution gene acting on a bay horse. Therefore, the buckskin is the extension, or the black base coat "E" gene, and the agouti "A" gene. It restricts the black base to the points and one copy of the crème gene that lightens the red/brown color to a gold/tan coat color. The buckskin body coat is predominantly a shade of yellow, ranging from gold to nearly brown. The points will be black or dark brown. True buckskins always have a dorsal stripe, shoulder stripe, and barring on the legs is always present. However, a dorsal stripe is not necessary for registration.

There are two Buckskin registries: the American Buckskin Registry Association and the International Buckskin Horse Association. Due to the fact this color occurs in most breeds of horse, their confirmation, weight, height, and temperament will vary with each horse. White markings are highly frowned upon in this breed of horse. The only permissible white is on the face and lower legs below the knee and hock. No white marks are admissible on the body. There are four colors recognized by the IBHA, listed below.

Dun: the body color differs only by the shade of color that is lighter.

Grulla: the body color is smoky blue or mouse-colored, with black points. The grulla (grew-yah) has no white hair mixed with dark hair, as seen in the roan or grey horse. Grulla comes from the Spanish word meaning "Blue Crane." White markings are also restricted.

Red Dun: the body coat is just that-red. Body color can vary from yellow to nearly flesh-colored. Points are dark red, and a dorsal stripe is necessary.

Buckskin dun: this type of horse carries the cream gene dilution and has a coat of pale gold with a black mane, tail, legs and primitive markings.

The Dun Horse: True dun horses should maintain primitive markings like the Tarpan and Przewalski's horses. The dun factor carries another dilution gene but not the cream gene. Primitive marking includes shoulder blade stripes, dorsal stripes, zebra stripes on the legs, and webbing.

Equestrian Activities

In the world today, there are many activities available for the horseman to participate. Below is a list of activities to expand a potential horse owner's knowledge before purchasing an Equine.

Trail Riding: The trail horse is one of the most common activities for the majority of horse owners. There are numerous events involving trail riding: for example, competitive endurance riding, trail classes in a horse show, and stock horse class competitions. Trail riding consists of a rider and horse working a series of obstacles over a period of time or in sequential order. The obstacles must be completed without fault and in some cases, a time schedule.

Western and English Pleasure: Here, the horses compete in horse shows. Pleasure classes are judged on the horse's ability to perform at the walk, jog (trot), and lope (canter). The horse should perform all three of these gaits with a free-flowing reasonable stride matching with its confirmation while exhibiting the accepted gaits and correct cadence. In both pleasure classes, the horse is the primary focus.

Halter: All breeds have set specific guidelines for breed confirmation. The halter class is designed for the sole purpose of exhibiting the ideal confirmation of a particular breed. For example, the ideal horse should possess eye appeal that has a harmonious blending, an attractive head, and a well-balanced body that corresponds with the breed types; individual characteristics. Confirmation is defined as the physical appearance due to the arrangement of muscle, bone, and other body tissues.

Jumping: Horses compete in events designed to test the animal's ability to jump different heights of obstacles in a designated series. The horse is judged on the ability to perform each jump with grace and ease without faults, meaning not knocking down any poles on the jump itself in sequential order. Jumpers compete for points, grace, and fluidity. Hunters compete for the speed of the event.

Dressage: The term dressage in French means "training." Its fundamental purpose is to develop, through standardized progressive training methods, a horse's natural athletic ability and willingness to perform, thereby maximizing its potential as a riding horse. Dressage has ancient roots, first recognized during the Renaissance. The great European riding masters developed a sequential training system that has changed little since then. Classical dressage is still considered the basis of trained modern dressage horses.

Cutting: Cutting originated from cattle ranches in the American West, where it was the cutting horse's job to separate cows from the herd for vaccination, castrating, or sorting. Eventually, competitions arose in arena situations in 1946. It is an equestrian event in the Western riding world where a horse and rider are judged on their ability to separate a cow from a cattle herd and keep it separate for a period of time.

Team Penning: The history of the sport dates back to 1942, when some cowboys reportedly came upon the idea of organizing what were routine cowboy chores, such as branding, doctoring, or transport, into a competitive sport.

This is a competition in which cowboys can showcase their horsemanship.

This is a Western sport where cattle are separated into pens by three riders on horseback. The riders are given sixty to seventy seconds to separate three same-numbered cattle from a herd of thirty and put them into a 16x24 pen through a ten-foot gate at the opposite end of the arena, which is usually located in the back side of the pen.

This is one of the fastest-growing sports in the Equine industry. The USTPA in Ft. Worth, Texas has an estimated 93,000 active team penners in North America.

Rodeo Events

Professional rodeo evolved from the working lifestyle of a cowboy. Today events carry on the rugged tradition established by their 19th-century predecessors, such as the Wild West shows produced by the legendary Buffalo Bill, who painted a colorful portrait of the working lifestyles of the frontiersman. The first Cowboys organized an association in 1936, calling it the Cowboys Turtle Association (CTA). There are several events included in today's rodeo about the Equine industry.

Bareback Bronc Riding places the cowboy in the middle of a 1,200-pound twisting, bucking tornado, and the aim is to make it through an eight-second ride. His only handhold is a piece of leather and rawhide rigging placed around the horse just behind its shoulders. If the rider is bucked off or touches the animal before eight seconds is up, he is disqualified.

Steer Wrestling is rodeo's most challenging test of leverage and strength. A contestant attempts to topple a steer averaging three to five times the bulldogger's weight. During the event, a rider called the Hazer runs parallel to the steer, keeping it running straight, while the steer wrestler must catch up to the steer, lean off the horse at top speed, and secure a firm grip on the horns. Once the rider is on the ground, the wrestler plants his feet and wrestles the steer to the ground. When the steer is on its side, with its feet facing the same direction, the time clock is stopped.

Team Roping is the only event that requires two competitors. The header ropes the steer's horns, and the heeler goes to work trying to catch the two hind feet. This is one of the most difficult maneuvers in rodeo competitions. After the ropers catch the cow, the ropes must be dallied around the horn, with the ropers facing each other, to stop the time. There is a ten-second penalty if the horse breaks the barrier and a five-second penalty if only one foot is caught.

Saddle Bronc Riding is the rodeo's classic event. This is an exercise in style and fitness that demands near-perfect timing between rider and horse. A rider must stay in the saddle for the usual eight seconds. To earn a high score, he must ride with the grace and fluidity of a dancer. A six-foot braided rein is held by one hand, and if the rider touches himself, the horse, or any equipment, he is disqualified. A perfect saddle bronc ride has never been earned; a high point ride is a score of one hundred.

Tie-Down Roping is one rodeo event that can be traced directly to ranch work. The calf gets a designated head start in the arena ahead of the horse. Once the cowboy and horse are in the arena, he must rope the calf, dismount, drop the three-hundred-pound calf, gather three legs in a "pigging" string, then throw his hands in the air for time to stop.

Barrel Racing is usually designated to women; however, anyone can compete. This event shows not only the rider's skill but the horse must be able to maneuver three barrels in a set pattern with speed and agility. Tipping a barrel over will cost the team five seconds. Barrel races have been won by just hundredths of a second.

The Purchase of a Horse

There are several steps to follow before the decision to purchase a horse is made. The next section is a checklist for the potential buyer to aid in the process of becoming a horse owner.

- ➢ The financial reserves available for the purchase, including, if necessary, training and riding instruction.
- ➢ Boarding costs, if necessary.
- ➢ Horse housing purchases, if necessary.
- ➢ Tack and equipment
- ➢ Feed costs
- ➢ Farrier or veterinarian expenses
- ➢ Purchase place examples:
- ➢ Reputable horse rescue facilities such as United Animal Friends, Humane Society, or ASPCA.
- ➢ An equestrian professional
- ➢ Newspaper
- ➢ Online horse sale websites
- ➢ Friends
- ➢ Referrals

Choosing the activities performed by the horse will enable the prospective buyer to better choose the correct horse. The previous list should allow the buyer to find several horses of interest. Before calling the horse owner or seller, make a list of questions to ask while on the phone, for example:

Re-affirm the horse's age, color, breed, and registration if registered. Ask for confirmation of the papers in the event of a purchase. If the horse is registered, ask for the registration number so you can research their identity verification. Ask for references, if applicable.

- ➢ Ask for health records
- ➢ Vaccinations history
- ➢ Shoeing records
- ➢ Health certificate
- ➢ Injury records
- ➢ Feed schedule and the horse's diet
- ➢ Training level
- ➢ Basic level
- ➢ Intermediate level
- ➢ Advanced or finished level
- ➢ Showing points or experience
- ➢ Where was the horse trained?

- ➢ Who trained the horse?
- ➢ When was the horse trained?
- ➢ How often is the horse ridden or exercised?
- ➢ Who handles and rides the horse?
- ➢ When can the buyer come to look at and ride the horse?

Once an appointment has been made to see the horse in person, there are several precautions the potential buyer must take to ensure their safety.

The potential buyer must be prepared before the appointment. The following list of tack should be purchased if needed: saddle, bridle, pad, halter, lead rope, and grooming equipment needed for the rider to ride and handle the horse. Do not assume the owner will have the proper equipment.

Have a notebook to hold important papers such as registration transfers, receipts, health records, and any other personal information needed. The financial paperwork should be to place a down payment or purchase the horse.

Research the registration forms by the breed registries to be aware of any fraudulent paperwork.

In some instances, a veterinarian may be needed for a vet check, which means examining the horse for its health condition and soundness. However, these health verifications are based on the veterinarian's visual perception. Tests and further exams are needed for concrete accuracy. Mistakes can be made, and problems can occur, even if there are no mistakes made by anyone in particular.

The final step in the equation is handling the horse in person. For example:

Observe the horse for obvious physical conditions like, weight, coat condition, injury scarring, and general appearance.

- Judge the horse's confirmation.
- What is the horse's mental status?
- Calm
- Nervous
- Aggressive
- Obstinate

One of the most important factors is judging if the horse has been tranquilized before the potential buyer's arrival. In the event the buyer suspects the horse has been drugged, contact a veterinarian immediately. Modern drugs are extremely difficult to observe visually. The horse should be alert to their surroundings and relaxed with a natural personality.

Examine the horse's feet and shoes for the level of care. The horse needs to be shod on all four feet if the horse needs shoes. Normally a horse that is wearing shoes only on the front feet is lacking in training. Pick the horse's feet up to inspect the condition of the frog and sole for thrush, bruising, punctures, and or other injuries.

The horse should be handled with assurance by the owner, not nervousness or aggression. This will determine the horse's mental status.

What is the condition of the owner's tack? The tack should be used but not worn or faulty. Horse tack should be kept in a tack room or horse trailer. This will determine the normal use of the horse.

Determine the owner's knowledge level, such as:

- The proper way to saddle and bridle a horse.
- Explain the horse's training level and the cues used to handle the horse.
- The handler should be honest about the horse regarding both its faults and assets.

Finally, the seller should be willing to lose a sale for the safety of the potential buyer.

In the event the buyer needs professional guidance for either training the horse or riding instruction, below are some guidelines to follow when choosing an equestrian professional.

> Experience
> Education
> Compassion
> Training Methods

The horse is a creature created by God, and in the proper environment, any horse can flourish. In situations when the horse is blamed for an accident, the only one that suffers is the horse.

Author Bio

Anna provides it all as if you are in the saddle along for the journey. Her rare books bring the readers joy from nearly every genre they can appreciate. She exuberantly brings the image and sentiments of the West to full life throughout the storyline. Yet, at the core of Judd's work is a black stallion who engages life in every aspect of the book. Haystack fills children's minds with wonder as he interacts with Marshal Spur and the Outrider Gang, to the mild-minored young steed who brings Adam to new levels of learning in his life. Then he is brilliantly portrayed as a beautiful Appaloosa stallion in the Broncobuster as Cash.

Anna is one of the greatest novelists, and a freelance ghostwriter known for equestrian professionalism in every genre. Her young adult fiction novels and all books bring joy to the readers.

Lizzy is the founder of Writers Publishing House/Ghost Writer Media, who writes under her pen name Anna Elizabeth Judd, a solid publishing firm with more than a decade of assisting clients will their publishing needs. She has a BA in fine arts with a minor in Equine Science. On the side, she studied at Scottsdale Art Institute under Robert 'Shoofly' Shufelt.

Lizzy writes books, which considering this website, makes perfect sense. She is best known for ghostwriting various best-sellers in all genres, along with her novels based on the initial part of her working career, horse training. As she understands the importance of family values, Lizzy chose a pen name borrowed from her family tree, Anna Elizabeth Judd.

When not absorbed in writing for clients, Lizzy can be found hiking, biking, or any outside activity. Although she does not train horses any longer, their spirits will always be a part of her soul. As a passionate entrepreneur Lizzy understands the importance of exemplary customer service; it is the basis for any successful business. In this case, Writers Publishing House was founded on the idea that the focus must be on the client's success. She believes, "Everyone should profit from their passion."

If you want to know more about publishing a book, please visit her website at https://writerspublishinghouse.com where you can contact her about starting your book project today.

Anna's Books: annaelizabethjudd.com

- The Power of Thought
- IAuthor – Social Media Marketing Guide
- The Handbook of Horsemanship
- The Broncobusters
- The Hourglass of el Diablo

- Marshal Spur and the Outlaw
- The Boy Who Couldn't Talk
- Spur Up! – Music Album
- Hey, Hay Learn Your ABCs
- Learn Your ABCs with Haystack

- A Distant Calling
- Skimmer's Adventure

Faith and Works

"What good is it, my brothers, if someone says he has faith but does not have works? Can that faith save him? If a brother or sister has nothing to wear and has no food for the day, and one of you says to them, 'Go in peace, keep warm, and eat well,' but you do not give them the necessities of the body, what good is it? So also, faith in itself, if it does not work, is dead. Indeed, someone might say, 'You have faith and I have works.' Demonstrate your faith to me without works, and I will demonstrate my faith to you with my works. You believe that God is one. You do well. Even the demons believe and tremble. Do you want proof, you ignoramus, that faith without works is useless? Was not Abraham our father justified by works when he offered his son Isaac upon the altar? You see that faith was active along with his works, and faith was completed by the works. Thus, the scripture was fulfilled that says, 'Abraham believed God and it was credited to him as righteousness,' and he was called 'the friend of God.' 'See how a person is justified by works and not faith alone. And in the same way, was not Rahab the harlot also justified by works when she welcomed the messengers and sent them out by a different route? For just as a body without spirit is dead, so also faith without works is dead." James 3;

www.ingramcontent.com/pod-product-compliance
Lightning Source LLC
Chambersburg PA
CBHW060246100726
47907CB00003B/783